On the page, he looked so happy with his frozen smile. The photo had been taken much earlier in the school year—months before Alex's death and Tess's departure.

I'm only going to look around, she thought, justifying her own actions to her conscience. *I just want to get an idea of what's going on in his head, so I can figure out what to do. There's nothing dangerous in that. I do it all the time.*

And yet, her own *sub*conscious was practically screaming out to her that this was not a good idea. *You should wait for your brother to get back,* the intense voice said to her.

Ignoring the inner voices, Isabel placed her right index finger on the photo of Kyle, concentrating on her subject. Closing her eyes, she willed herself into her friend's dreams. Her body relaxed as she could feel her mind leaving on its journey. Slumping down into the bed, the yearbook slipped out of her hands and fell onto the floor.

ROSWELL™

DREAMWALK

PAUL RUDITIS

From the television series
developed by Jason Katims

SIMON PULSE
New York   London   Toronto   Sydney   Singapore

This book is a work of fiction. Any references to historical events, real people, or real locales are used fictitiously. Other names, characters, places, and incidents are the product of the author's imagination, and any resemblance to actual events or locales or persons, living or dead, is entirely coincidental.

First Simon Pulse edition January 2003

™ and © 2003 Twentieth Century Fox Film Corporation, Regency Entertainment (USA) Inc. and Monarchy Enterprises B.V.

SIMON PULSE
An imprint of Simon & Schuster
Children's Publishing Division
1230 Avenue of the Americas
New York, NY 10020

Printed in the United States of America
10 9 8 7 6 5 4 3 2 1

Library of Congress Control Number 2002107315

ISBN 0-689-85518-4

For L. J., Tim, Shawn, and John

PROLOGUE

Knifing through the desert for mile after mile he passed nothing but desolate land. An open road lay out before him and miles of road behind. Looking back, he saw nothing but knew they were there. He wasn't sure if he was running away from something or heading toward it, but he knew for certain that he did not have much time.

You did this to me. You sent me to Las Cruces.

He was not alone. True, the voices in his mind accompanied him wherever he was going, but there was something else . . . *someone* else. The additional presence was both calming and disturbing at the same time.

But the voices . . . they were there too . . . always.

Alex, Alex, let me fix your mind. You're not thinking straight.

The car pulled to the side of the road. The sun beat down and reflected off mile marker forty-seven, burning into his eyes. Stepping out of the passenger side onto the parched desert land, he waited in the searing heat.

You mindwarped me for two months . . . now there's nothing left. . . . You destroyed my mind!

1

A pair of vultures circled overhead. Their meandering course persisted on above. His eyes were drawn to watch them, though he wanted to look away. It was only a matter of time before they attacked. He knew that for certain. The attack always came. But he did not fear for his own safety. They only fought each other.

Kyle get out. Kyle go!

He was back in his bedroom, encircled by the wood paneling he had tried to cover with posters of heroes in his youth. Heroes he had often hoped would come in and save him from his life. Heroes he now knew did not have the power for the kind of rescue he required.

I have nothing. I might as well be dead!

The voices persisted as shadows danced around him. First looming indistinct ghosts of a past long gone, followed by more recent wraiths who began to find flesh and form. First she appeared, looking so harmless, yet hiding within her an unimaginable evil. Then he emerged, the helpless innocent fearing for his own life and sanity. Fearing her.

Calm down. Calm down!

No, you can't mindwarp me!

An old friend. A new enemy. Surrounding him. Trapping him. Drawing ever closer. His mind hurt. The pain was excruciating. He tried to block it out, to run from it, but he could not move.

You can't mindwarp me. . . . No!!! Nooooo!!!

Kyle bolted up in his bed, sweat soaking through his T-shirt as he held tight to the covers on the unseasonably cool summer night. His eyes adjusted to the darkness as the shadows lessened and familiar forms began to take shape around his bed.

Visually exploring the room that he had reclaimed after Tess's departure, Kyle knew that he was alone, but not entirely. Hardly a night had gone by in the past several weeks that he was not haunted by the images. What he had once forgotten, he was forced to remember, and since the day he recalled the mindwarp that Tess had performed on him, he could not escape the memory.

He had witnessed Alex's death at Tess's hands and had unwittingly taken part in the cover-up. He'd then attended his friend's funeral unaware of his own involvement in the murder. He'd even comforted Tess and sought comfort from her as they had continued to form a familial bond like that of a brother and sister. She had been the closest friend he'd had in a long time, but eventually he discovered that it had all been a lie.

Since the day Liz and Maria had helped him remember everything, his dreams had been full of voices of the past. The images of the horrific act plagued his mind as other, more confusing thoughts raced through his head. He saw a combination of things familiar and unusual. But, even worse, the images remained even afterward, and the voices followed him when he awoke.

First his own voice.

You want me to come along?

And then hers.

No. Go in the house. I'll take care of everything from here.

1

"**A**re you sure you want to do this?" Max asked a question he had asked often in the past two years with the same intensity he usually reserved for life-and-death situations.

"I've come this far," Liz replied, looking unsure. "Everyone is counting on me."

"They'll understand," he said.

"But I won't." Liz stepped out of the booth, smoothing the wrinkles in her light blue dress. She had chosen the color after making the rule that no one was to wear black that night. Black was morbid. Tonight was a celebration of life. "I was so busy trying to solve Alex's murder that I never had the chance to let him go. I have to do this. Not just for Alex, but for myself."

Dressed in a rust-colored T-shirt with brown pants, Max watched as Liz walked through the small crowd at the Crashdown, heading for the makeshift stage they had set up in front of the counter. It was little more than a few lights and a microphone borrowed from the school AV closet, but it was going to have to do. Max thought it was great of Liz's father to forgo a night's profits and close down the café for the gathering of friends and family.

The group included their own inner circle, minus Kyle, who was finishing up at his new job at the auto shop. There were also some of Alex's closer friends from school—the lucky students of West Roswell High whose main concerns in life had to do with grades and finding a date for Saturday night and not life-and-death alien encounters. Max knew most of them fairly well, but could not count them as close friends since his very nature kept him distant from anyone for fear of bringing them into his life like he had brought in Liz and her friends. And tonight was a perfect example of why that was such a horrible thing for him to do to them.

Aside from friends, he counted many families among the participants. His own adoptive parents were there, supporting him, Isabel, and the Whitmans as they had a couple months ago at the funeral. Maria's mom was there too, sitting at a table next to Sheriff Valenti. Even though the sheriff had lost his job helping Max, he couldn't think of the man as anything other than "sheriff." Seeing the two single parents together, their strange, shared history of being abandoned by their spouses years ago inexplicably popped into Max's head. Ignoring the thought, Max continued scanning the room, ending with Alex's parents. He didn't even want to think about what they were going through.

"It started four years ago," Liz spoke into the microphone. "It was during my short-lived artistic phase, before I really got into science. Alex, Maria, and I got together on this midsummer's night to have our own private talent show. Alex and Maria played bass and guitar while they sang, and I did whatever I could to keep up with them, mostly by reciting some poetry." She took a breath to choke back on the tears that were about to escape. "We continued the tradition every summer since, and now I invite you all to join in with us, in memory of Alex."

Max saw that Maria was already dabbing her eyes with a tissue. He almost laughed in spite of the somber mood, because her outfit was truly priceless. She had totally embraced Liz's color directive and was wearing a rainbow-colored sequin minidress that he had actually helped her pick out at a local thrift shop. The two of them had really bonded as friends the previous summer and still spent a lot of time together when their significant others were otherwise engaged.

"I'd like to start off tonight with a poem that I know was very dear to Alex," Liz continued as she picked up a book left on the counter and opened it to the page still marked by a pair of concert tickets. "It's called 'Stopping by Woods on a Snowy Evening.'" She looked out at the crowd at each of her friends, finally stopping on Alex's parents as she read, "'Whose woods these are I think I know. . . .'"

As Max listened, he also settled his eyes on Alex's parents and gave himself permission to try to imagine what they could possibly be feeling. To have their son taken at such a young age was something he could only partially wrap his head around. Though his own son was millions of miles from him, the Whitmans' pain was different from his own. Their suffering came after raising a child for seventeen years only to have his life ended in a seemingly senseless accident. It made Max feel even worse to think that they would always assume that their son had taken his own life, and would never know the truth.

He turned his full attention back to Liz, thinking how beautiful and fragile she looked under the spotlight reading from Alex's book. She had been through so much since her close friend's death, and now that Tess was finally out of the picture, Max promised himself that he would do whatever he could to make things up to her, starting with being there for her on this very important night.

" . . . 'And miles to go before I sleep,'" Liz finished the poem openly crying, finally letting out all the grief she had been holding in since the day she had gotten her first clue to Alex's death.

Max was quickly out of his seat and by her side, escorting Liz to a chair. "Alex would have liked this," he whispered.

Liz was speechless as she sat down in the booth, her body slightly trembling.

Polite applause filled the Crashdown as Liz's own parents looked on, openly concerned for their daughter but apparently content to know that Max was by her side.

Alex's former band mates were next on the bill. They were setting up their equipment in the staging area to do a set in honor of their missing bass player. This would be the last time they would be performing together under the name "The Whits," and each member thought this was the appropriate time and place for such a performance.

Alex had brought the group together sophomore year in deference to the fact that the Roswell garage band scene was rather pitiful. He was the driving force behind the band, as evidenced by the name they had settled on. Even though Maria had temporarily hijacked the group soon after their creation, Alex had always been the one in charge. As the guys began their first melancholy song of lost love, which had been written by Alex, Isabel came over to join her brother and Liz.

"Are you sure you know your lines?" she whispered to Max as she sat in the booth. She had also taken Liz's wardrobe instructions to heart and was wearing a pale orange dress to fit in with the "celebration of life" theme of the evening.

"Yes, Isabel," Max said, for the tenth time since having agreed to perform the skit with her. "I'm sure I know my lines."

"I just don't want you to freeze up in the middle," she explained.

"Relax," he calmly replied. "We'll be fine."

"Do you want to go rehearse again in the back?" she asked, getting up before he could answer.

Liz looked to Max, begging him with her eyes not to leave her alone right now. He reached to his side and took her hand in his, giving it a squeeze to let her know that he wouldn't be going anywhere.

With his other hand, Max grabbed his sister by the arm and lightly tugged her back down into the booth across from him. "We've rehearsed it a hundred times. It's going to be fine. Stay here and enjoy the music."

"I just . . ." She had a catch in her throat.

"I know."

As Max held on to Liz with his hand, he locked eyes

with his sister, letting her know that he was there for her, too. Silently, Max provided the necessary support for the two girls who, in addition to Maria, were probably closer to Alex than any other students at West Roswell High.

All three of them fought back tears as the mournful tune filled the Crashdown. It even looked to Max like the band was about to lose it at any moment. Somehow, this "celebration of life," had gotten off to a rather depressing start. But Max wasn't quite sure how to go about turning things around.

"This is ridiculous," Liz said from out of nowhere. "This is supposed to be a joyous occasion."

"Well, Liz, you're the one setting the tone," Max gently reminded her, still providing her the strength she would need to take charge of the event.

"Exactly," she stood and crossed over to the lead guitarist, Mickey, as the band finished their heavyhearted tune. Max watched as she whispered something into Mickey's ear that immediately made his face light up and his head nod vigorously. As Liz returned to the table, Max watched as the guitarist relayed the message to the rest of the band. Each member looked more pleased than the next as they readied their instruments.

"Ladies and gentlemen," Mickey addressed the crowd, "we've had a special request." He bowed his head toward Liz in gratitude.

"Let's dance," Liz said as she pulled Max from his seat.

On cue, the band started up again, and Max recognized another one of their tunes. This time, however, the song was much faster. Taking their lead, Maria got up in her shimmering rainbow outfit and hopped up to the microphone, letting loose on the song that she remembered from her days fronting the band. Soon the whole place was rocking and everyone was out of their seats, including Alex's mom, who was dancing with Sheriff Valenti. There was, however, one person who was still in his chair.

"I don't think Mr. Whitman dances," Max said as he nodded his head in the direction of Alex's father while keeping the beat.

"Oh, you'd be surprised," Liz said with a laugh. "You should have seen him when he chaperoned the sixth-grade dance. He taught me some moves I'd never seen before or have been able to do since. Will you excuse me?"

Max nodded politely as Liz left him to go to Mr. Whitman. At first, Alex's father was reluctant to join in the festivities, but Liz flashed the charming smile that Max knew from personal experience no man could resist, no matter what his age or marital status.

Soon enough, Mr. Whitman was up on the dance floor. Feeling awkward as the only one on the dance floor standing alone, Max noticed there was one other person in the diner who was not dancing, and went back to the kitchen to join him.

"Are you going to watch from back here all night, Michael?" Max asked as he stepped into the kitchen.

"It's the safest place to be in case Maria makes a scene," Michael replied as he tended to the grill.

"You should go easy on her," Max said, leaning against the counter. "This has got to be difficult."

"Which is exactly why I'm staying in the kitchen," Michael replied.

Max honestly wanted to delve into the latest drama in

the Michael/Maria relationship, but he didn't think he had enough energy left. Providing emotional support for Liz and Isabel was draining enough for Max, especially considering that he still blamed himself for Alex's death.

In the past months, dozens of "what ifs" had gone through his head as he'd tried to figure out a way he could have changed events so things wouldn't have turned out the way they had. But Max knew he could not alter the past as much as he knew that he could not tell what the future had in store for him and his friends. There was so much on Max's mind as he watched the party through the kitchen's service window that he almost couldn't concentrate on any one thing at all.

"You and Liz okay now?" Michael asked when he noticed the direction in which Max's gaze was fixed.

"Oh, sure," Max replied, keeping his eyes locked onto the dance floor. "We're closer than we've been in a long time."

"So what's with the look?" Michael persisted.

"It's Mr. Whitman," Max said as he caught an actual expression of happiness creep onto the face of Alex's dad for the first time that evening. Mr. Whitman was lifting Liz up into the air, doing some amazing moves that Max had only seen in movies. "I don't know how he does it."

"Does what?" Michael asked. "Dance?"

Max had to chuckle in spite of his mood. Michael always appeared to miss the subtleties of life, which often proved to be a sore point in his relationship with Maria, but Max knew that his friend caught on to things far more often than he showed. "I don't know how he goes on with his life," Max explained. "He raised Alex, and now his son is gone. How does a father cope with it?"

"Doesn't seem like he has much of a choice," Michael said as he continued to flip burgers. "It has been a couple months since Alex died." Then he added, "And since Tess left."

"That's not what this is about," Max said.

"Isn't it?" Michael asked, already knowing the answer. "Your son's probably been born by now, right?"

"If Tess was telling the truth when she said her alien pregnancy would only last a month," Max reluctantly conceded, "then, yes, I have a son."

"We'll get him back, Maxwell," Michael said, ignoring the food for a moment. He put his hand on his friend and leader's shoulder to stress his words. "I promise you."

"I know," Max agreed without a doubt in his mind. "But then what?"

"Then we raise him," Michael replied.

"You and me?" Max asked, only partially joking. "How do I raise a hybrid human/alien child? I'm a child myself."

"Max, you haven't been a kid since we came out of the pods when we were six," Michael reminded him. "You've been an adult your entire life. Hell, you were an adult even *before* this life."

"It's just . . . ," Max started.

"Are you going to hide in here all night?" Maria asked accusingly as she blew into the kitchen with Liz trailing her silver platform heels. Her song apparently over, Max assumed that she was probably angry her boyfriend had missed hearing her sing.

"I'm helping Max deal with his intense issues over fatherhood," Michael said, largely to change the subject to get Maria off the path that she was about to take him down once again.

"Thanks, Michael," Max said, wishing that his personal issues could have remained personal for just a while longer. Immediately, he saw a familiar look of concern in Liz's eyes. He had been hoping to spare her his problems for at least this night. Max tried not to get angry with Michael for using their private conversation as a distraction for Maria, but it wasn't easy.

"Besides," Michael added. "I'm cooking."

"Looks done to me," Maria said as she eyed the burgers. "Well-done, in fact. Come on, we can bring the food out while my mom does her Earth Mother performance art piece."

"Can't miss that," Michael sarcastically replied as he started flipping the burgers onto some buns. Maria helped out by removing the French fries from the deep fryer and pouring them onto a serving platter. Silence hung in the room as they finished getting the food ready, and Liz waited to follow up on the question she had been wanting to ask since she and Maria walked into the room to Michael's less than warm response.

With all the food on its respective serving trays, Michael and Maria silently made their way out to the dining room area, leaving their friends behind in the kitchen.

"Do you want to talk about it?" Liz asked as soon as the kitchen door swung closed.

"Not tonight," Max said. "Tonight, I get to be here for you for once instead of the other way around."

There was a pause as Max's words hung in the air.

"Okay, we both know *that's* not going to work," Liz said, smiling at him. "So why don't you just cut to the chase and tell me what's wrong?"

"Why can't anyone just let me wallow in my pain?" Max asked rhetorically.

"Because the last time you did that, you got drunk with Kyle off one sip of alcohol and totally crashed my blind date from Hell," Liz said, reminding him of one of his less than stellar evenings from well over a year ago. "Spill it."

"Just having some fatherly regrets," he said.

"We'll get him back," Liz said, mustering up support for him even though she was talking about a child that he shared with Tess.

"Like I told Michael, that's not the problem." Once again, his gaze leaped to Mr. Whitman, who was still on the dance floor twirling his wife in circles.

"It's what to do with him once he gets here?" Liz correctly assumed.

"I look at Alex's dad and I can't imagine dealing with that kind of pain," Max said. "His son was living this life that he knew nothing about and eventually it killed him, and his father will never know the truth."

"Maybe someday—," Liz started hopefully.

"Then I think of me and my dad," Max unintentionally cut her off. "Things are never going to be truly honest between us, because I can't share with him the most important part of my life. Even so, I know when I need him, he'll be there for me. I don't know if I have that kind of strength."

"Of course you do," Liz said.

"Do I?" Max truly wondered. "Think of Sheriff Valenti raising Kyle on his own. The two of them are so close. Will I ever be that close to my son?"

"Kyle's mom left them over a decade ago," Liz reminded him. "They didn't have a choice. They only had each other."

"How am I ever going to have that kind of bond with my son after I get him back from his mother—a woman who murdered one of our closest friends? How do I explain everything to him when I don't understand it myself?"

Max knew that Liz was holding her feelings for Alex at bay so she could help him with his problem, and the knowledge was making him feel even worse.

"I don't know," she said honestly. "But I do know that you'll make a great dad. You're a born leader. Literally. How hard could fatherhood be compared with ruling a planet?"

"That's a bit of a jump," Max said.

"True, but it's the best I can do right now." Liz's face lit up. "Hey, I've got an idea. For once, we have a conveniently timed crisis. My parents arranged for me to go to Artesia this weekend to baby-sit their friends' son Jason while his parents go out of town. Why don't you come along? It will give you a chance to spend some time in charge of a twelve-year-old boy."

"I don't think our parents would like us spending the weekend alone together," Max reminded her.

"So we don't tell them," Liz said. "It certainly won't be the first secret we've kept from them. And we won't be alone. Jason will be there, and he won't say anything to anyone."

"I don't know."

"Doesn't matter," Liz replied bluntly. "You're going."

As if to add a formal end to their conversation, Michael came back into the kitchen. "Max, your sister's looking for you," he said, carrying the now empty serving trays. "Has Liz solved your problem yet?"

"Almost," Liz replied. "I was just . . ."

But before she could finish her sentence, the back door slammed open and shut.

Concerned, Liz, Max, and Michael moved from the kitchen to the back room. There, they found Kyle still wearing his blue work overalls, breathing heavily and looking rather pale.

"Wow," Michael said. "You look like crap."

2

"There you are," Isabel exclaimed with relief as she found her brother in the back room. "Come on, we're up next." She plopped a baseball cap on his head and grabbed him by the arm.

"Isabel, wait," he tried to say, but she ignored him.

"Whatever end-of-the-world situation we're in the middle of, it can wait." She pulled him to the door. "We're doing this."

It was now the time for Isabel to pay her respects to the one boy who had truly loved her, even though she had pushed him aside—not because she didn't want him, but because she didn't want him to be hurt. But he had been hurt—*killed*—and since she couldn't change the past, she was going to do her best to honor him in the present.

"Isabel—," Kyle started to say as she pushed the still swinging door back open.

"Hey, Kyle," she replied before he could say anything else. "Glad you made it in time for our skit." Then she and Max were out of the kitchen.

"I'm not going to miss this one," Michael said as he followed.

Alone with her ex-boyfriend, Liz asked the obvious: "What's wrong?"

"Nothing," he replied unconvincingly.

"Are you sure?" she asked. "Michael was right. You don't look too well."

"Lack of sleep," he replied curtly. "We should get out there." Kyle didn't give Liz a chance to respond and he headed out to the café part of the Crashdown and took a seat with his dad.

Isabel stepped into the glow of the small spotlight that was also borrowed from the school AV closet. She had gone to the school over the weekend with Max and Michael to pick everything up. Granted, it hadn't actually been a faculty sanctioned visit to the school, nor did they technically have permission to borrow the equipment, but it was for a good cause. Besides, with classes out for the summer, they didn't know how else to get inside, and they fully intended to return the equipment before anyone would even miss it.

Wearing a baseball cap of her own, she waited while her brother helped Ms. DeLuca clean the glitter, confetti, and pork rinds that she had spilled out during her performance art piece. It had been actually a poignant tribute, although Isabel still didn't understand how the pork rinds fit in.

Using the extra time, Isabel went over the routine in her head once again. She had convinced her brother to perform the comedy skit with her by explaining that Alex had loved old-time vaudeville comedians, especially

Abbott and Costello. He had even managed to drag Isabel to the annual Roswell Weekend Classic Comedy Movie Marathon at the Palace Theatre last year. He had always been trying to get her to see classic cinema, and she was glad now that at least once, she had given in to him. At first, she had questioned her own idea to do a comedy sketch at a memorial service, but Liz had supported her by agreeing that it totally fit in with the evening's theme. In tribute, she chose Abbott and Costello's famous "Who's on First?" routine to perform for the group.

Ms. Deluca had finally managed to get all the remnants of her performance off the floor, which allowed for Isabel to step up to the microphone. She took a deep breath before speaking her memorized introduction.

"Alex loved to laugh," she said to the crowd of friends. "Even in times of crisis, he would come up with some totally out-of-place comment that would always break the tension. With that in mind, my brother and I would like to perform one of his favorite comedy routines, altered slightly to meet the abilities of the performers."

Taking a moment to get accustomed to the audience, Isabel couldn't help but wish that there were a couple more familiar faces looking on. Naturally, she missed Alex and wanted him back more than anything, but she had also hoped that Jesse Ramirez could have been there as well.

She had only recently begun dating the handsome young lawyer from her dad's firm, but somehow she knew that they were destined to be together forever. Of course, forever was going to have to wait until such time that she could actually tell someone they were dating. Things were just too complicated right now for her to explain that she was falling in love with someone while still mourning Alex's death. And things would be even more complicated when the time came that she would have to introduce Jesse into her crazy alien life. For now, she wanted to enjoy her time as a recent high school graduate and the life of a seemingly normal teen. As long as she and Jesse kept their secret, she would always have one very important part of her life that was blissfully normal.

"So . . . I recently bought a baseball team," Max said, standing beside her on the makeshift stage.

Immediately pulled from her musings into the real world, Isabel caught the end of her brother's cue. "Oh really," she said. "I *love* baseball players. So, tell me the names of the guys on your team."

"Well," Max said as he began the comedic part of the classic skit. "*Who's* on first—"

"That's what I want to know," Isabel interrupted, pretending to be confused.

"And that's why I'm telling you," Max said in a mock stern voice. "If you'll just listen to me."

"Okay," Isabel replied. "Who's on first?"

"Exactly." Max gave a sharp nod of his head.

Isabel squinted her eyes in an effort to act confused. "What?"

"He's on second," Max replied.

"Who's on second?" Isabel asked.

"No," Max corrected her with a forced tone of annoyance. "*Who's* on first." They received their first restrained chuckle from the audience. Somehow dancing came easier than laughing, but they were beginning to get into the routine.

"I don't know!" Isabel replied, pretending to get annoyed.

"He's on third base," Max said to the first real laugh from the audience.

Isabel loved hearing the laughter because it made everything all right for at least a little while. More importantly, she finally got the joke herself. When Alex had dragged her to the classic movie marathon she had laughed at the funny parts, but she'd never really understood why laughing was so important. In her life, between being chased by the FBI and fighting off an attack from the Skins, there often seemed so little to laugh about. She finally understood the power of humor and why Alex always seemed to have a joke or a lighthearted comment ready just when she needed it most.

But as she looked out to the crowd, she realized that someone wasn't laughing. At first, she had noticed Kyle because he seemed to be nodding off during the show. Not only did Kyle look like he was struggling to stay awake during their skit, but he seemed intent on it, and not just for the sake of being polite. *What's going on with Kyle?* she asked herself. *He has a look of . . . terror?*

Isabel made a mental note to ask him about it later, because she needed to concentrate on the last bit of wordplay involved or else she was going to blow the joke entirely.

"So, let me get this straight," she said, gearing up for the finale. "The ball is thrown to *Who*. But, whoever it is at first drops the ball and the runner heads to second. So, *Who* picks up the ball and throws it to *What*. *What* throws it to *I Don't Know*. *I Don't Know* throws it back to *Tomorrow*.

Triple play. Then, say another guy gets up and hits a long fly ball to *Because*. Why? *I don't know*! He's on third and I don't give a darn!

"What?" Max asks, going in for the capper.

"I said I don't give a darn!" Isabel replied, acting exhausted by it all.

"Oh, that's our shortstop."

Uproarious laughter filled the Crashdown, and Isabel found herself giggling right along with everyone. The evening was turning out to be just what they all needed. A night to remember Alex fondly, without alien worries interfering. They had come together to provide support for one another as they began to distance themselves from Alex's death. Although he would never be forgotten, this was the right time for his friends to start the healing and eventual moving on. Everyone seemed to be having a great time.

Everyone but Kyle.

Making their way out of the spotlight, Isabel and her brother accepted the adulation and pats on the back from their audience. Liz stepped up to hug Max, giving him the kind of warm kiss that Isabel had not seen them share in quite some time. For the briefest moment, she was jealous of the fact that she couldn't be so public with the guy she was seeing. But, the trade-off for her clandestine relationship with Jesse was well worth the few pangs of regret.

Setting her sites on Kyle, Isabel continued through the crowd as the band took the stage for another short set. Kyle was looking down at his glass of soda, transfixed by it. Beside the glass, his fingers drummed a repetitive beat.

Tap, tap, tap. Tap, tap.

Tap, tap, tap. Tap, tap.

Isabel remembered when Liz explained that the tapping fingers were some kind of side effect experienced by people that Tess had mindwarped. It had happened to Maria's mom after Tess had forced her to forget a particularly confusing evening at the UFO Center. When Ms. DeLuca had started to remember things, her fingers would drum on the counter. It had also happened when Kyle remembered the horrible things that Tess had made him forget. But Maria had been keeping tabs on her mom, and reported that Ms. DeLuca had stopped tapping her fingers weeks ago. *Why hasn't Kyle?*

"So what, your soda's more interesting than our skit?" Isabel asked, smiling.

Apparently unaware of the fact that she was speaking to him, Kyle took a moment before he looked up at her. "Oh, no . . . no. I was just . . . thinking."

"Is something wrong?" she asked, about to take a seat.

"Yes," he replied, standing. "Can we go somewhere and talk?"

Without waiting for an answer, Kyle started heading for the back of the café as the band struck up yet another cheerful tune. They had exhausted their entire repertoire of original songs in the first set and had moved on to top-forty hits. Oddly, however, Maria had not joined them again.

Dutifully, Isabel followed Kyle, concerned for her friend. Unfortunately, when the pair walked into the back room of the Crashdown, they came right in on the middle of another one of Michael and Maria's love spats, which explained the singer's momentary absence from the stage.

"And look at your jeans!" Maria said in a tone of voice that was just short of yelling, not wanting to disturb the party in the other room.

"Oh, now you're going to insult my clothing?" Michael shot back in his usual sarcastic, defeatist tone.

"Black!" she slammed her locker door for effect. "It was the one color Liz specifically asked us not to wear. And look at you. Black jeans. Was it that difficult of a rule to understand? Should I have brought a color wheel by to explain what would have been an appropriate hue?"

"Sorry I don't own an extensive wardrobe," he said by way of an explanation. "I wore what was clean. Besides, I think you're wearing enough colors in that outfit for the both of us."

"I'm sorry," Kyle mumbled as he started to back out the door.

Isabel, however, was having none of that tonight. "Can't you two just put your petty little arguments on hold for one evening? It's really gotten way past the point of cute lovers' quarrels. Maria, why don't you go out there and sing some more with the band. Michael, you go watch her."

Without another word, Michael and Maria left the room in a huff. As soon as they were out the door, Isabel laughed to herself. "Some people express their love for each other in the strangest ways."

"Yeah," was the only response Kyle could muster.

"Okay, Kyle, spill it."

He took a deep breath, as if stalling for time to either convince himself to speak or to brace himself for Isabel's reaction for what he was about to say. "You remember the time you took me on a dreamwalk into the mind of the Playboy Playmate of the Year?" Kyle asked.

Isabel was afraid to think about where this one was going. "Yes. Afterward, I couldn't bathe long enough to make me feel clean after I realized the things you had in mind."

"I've been thinking a lot about that lately," he said, with no trace of lecherous teenage humor in his voice. His fingers were tapping against Liz's metal locker.

Tap, tap, tap. Tap, tap.

"I'm sure you have," Isabel said, taking his hand so that the metal-amplified drumming would stop. "But we won't be doing that again. I don't usually bring guests with me when I dreamwalk."

"That's not what I want."

"Then what, Kyle?" Isabel checked through the door's window to make sure none of the "out of the loop" guests was going to stumble across their conversation. It was more out of habit than concern. "What's with the mood you're in? I mean, obviously we're all upset, but you seem to be really agitated at the moment. I didn't think you and Alex were all that close."

"Right now, I feel closer to him than I think anyone else could," Kyle replied in a monotone. "I did kill him, after all."

A flood of denials came rushing to Isabel's mind. It was just a matter of which one would come out of her mouth first. "That's ridiculous. Tess killed him. You had nothing to do with it."

"But if I hadn't come into the room," he explained, "if I hadn't opened the door when I did, maybe Tess wouldn't have been pushing so hard on Alex's mind. She was trying to get him to shut up in front of me. She killed him because of me."

Isabel took a moment to gather her thoughts. She wasn't prepared to handle such a conversation, but knew that what she was about to say would carry a lot of weight with him. "And if I hadn't introduced Alex to Tess, it wouldn't have happened. And if Liz hadn't told him our secret, it wouldn't have happened. And if our spaceship had crashed in Tupelo, Mississippi, it wouldn't have happened. Kyle, there are millions of things that could have been done to avoid it, but none of us has the power to see the future. We can't stop things before they happen."

"But you can change things after the fact," Kyle replied. "You can make *people* change."

Isabel knew what he was talking about. "Kyle, Tess mindwarped you into helping her set up Alex's death. You didn't know what you were doing."

"I loaded him into the car like he was a duffel bag," Kyle reminded her.

"Because you *thought* he *was*," she shot back. "You had no control over your actions. She was using you."

"That's not much consolation," he replied. "Buddha says, 'Kill not, but have regard for life.'"

Isabel didn't have a good response to that one, so she went with the obvious. "I really don't care what Buddha says. I truly doubt that Buddha ever considered alien mind tricks when coming up with life philosophies."

She managed to elicit a slight smile from Kyle on that one. But it was quickly wiped away. In the momentary pause that followed, they both listened to the music coming from the restaurant. Apparently, Maria had taken Isabel's suggestion and once again had joined in with the band. She was wrapping up a tune by the group Save Ferris. It was a band Isabel knew Alex had loved.

"Kyle, why are you telling all this to me?" Isabel asked.

"I've been having trouble sleeping," he said. "I keep replaying the memory of Alex's death. Every time I close my eyes, I see myself walking in on them. Sometimes, I see myself in Alex's place. Other times, I see things that have nothing to do with it. Strange things that I don't understand."

"What kinds of things?"

"Everything," he replied. "And nothing, too. I can't explain it."

"So that's why you look so tired."

"It's not just when I'm sleeping," he continued. "This afternoon, I was working on a car when I got flashes of Alex's car hitting the truck. Isabel, I wasn't even there when the collision happened."

But Isabel knew what he was talking about, because she had seen it too. She thought it had been normal for the imagination to make them see these things. "I think that's just our minds trying to explain things. Since we weren't witnesses, our minds are making up the scenario so we can find some kind of closure."

"It's not closure," he said, sure of himself. "It's getting worse. Much worse."

"How?"

"It started out as just some nightmares and daydreams," he explained. "Normal grieving stuff. But now I can't get my mind off it. No matter what I do, I just keep seeing things that I have no control over."

"So, what can I do?" she asked, cautiously.

"Well, since the problem is dream related," Kyle began his pitch, "I was thinking maybe you could go in there and fix things."

"Fix your dreams?" she asked for clarification, because she wasn't exactly sure what he was proposing.

Kyle sensed her reluctance. "You've manipulated dreams before. I'd just go to sleep, and you would pop into my head and remove all the images of Alex's death."

"That's not manipulating dreams," Isabel said. "That's displacing memories. When I go into someone's dreams, it's purely harmless recreation. I'm only playing around with the dream. This is . . . different."

"But, Tess—"

"Has entirely different powers than I do," she reminded him. "I can't just go in and change your thoughts."

"Have you ever tried?" he asked, suspecting that he knew the answer.

"No."

"Then how do you—"

"It's too dangerous," she stopped him before he continued down this track. "We have no idea what that could do to you. It's just too dangerous."

"I'm willing to take that risk," he said. "I have nothing left to lose."

"Alex died," she said flatly. "He died because Tess went too far with her powers. I'm not going to do the same thing."

"But it's the only way," Kyle said.

"Have you even considered some kind of therapy?" Isabel said. "Maybe something more interactive than speaking to Buddha?"

"I would love to talk to someone about this," his agitation level was rising. "Tell me who. Tell me what therapist on Earth I can talk to and explain that I'm plagued by images in a murder I took part in because an alien messed with my mind. I would love to get normal help, but *normal* and *Roswell* don't mix."

Isabel couldn't argue that fact. She, Max, and Michael had lived with the secret all their lives. They'd known pretty much from the start that they were different. But their friends were pulled into their crazy lives, and now everyone's concept of normal had been thrown completely upside down. Isabel couldn't help but feel that she owed Kyle, but she also knew that she couldn't risk his life. "I'm sorry," she whispered. "I can't."

The statement hung in the air for the longest time as music continued to waft in from the other room. Kyle and Isabel just stared at each other, until finally the moment was broken by something entirely unexpected. Apparently, Maria had taken a break from performing with the band.

"Is that my dad?" Kyle asked as they listened to the impossible. "Is he . . . singing?"

3

"**S**hould we go over it one more time?" Max asked as he threw an extra shirt into his overnight bag.

His sister let out an audible sigh as she replayed the story for a third time that morning. "You and Michael are going to Frazier Woods for the entire weekend to do some stupid science project on plant life native to New Mexico so that Michael can make up for all the work he missed cutting classes during the school year. Really, dear brother, this is one of the easier cover stories we've ever had to come up with. I think I can manage it."

"I just don't want them to think something's up," Max said, zipping his bag closed. "We give them enough to worry about."

"Mom and Dad are driving to Santa Fe first thing tomorrow morning and are staying there overnight," Isabel reminded him. "I doubt they'll even notice you're gone."

"It's just," he tried to put his concern into words, "they already think Liz and I got too intense too fast. I don't want them to worry about us spending the weekend together, especially since we're not really spending it *alone* together."

Isabel opened the curtains in her brother's room to let in some of the morning sunlight. They were lucky that Friday was looking like it was going to be as nice as the rest of the week had been. Roswell was experiencing an unusual stretch of mild weather in the regularly hot summer.

"Oh," Max said, remembering one more thing. "Make sure Michael doesn't accidentally show up here. He knows what's going on, but sometimes with him I never know how much he's paying attention."

"You'll have to remember all this when your own son's a teenager," Isabel chided him. "I think this is the best lesson for dealing with a problem teen. 'What to do when you think your son's lying to you.'"

"Very funny," he said, although he knew that he was making more out of his sneaking off than necessary. He knew that she was right to treat him like he was overreacting, but having to lie to his parents never got any easier. At least this time he was hiding normal teenage stuff from them instead of huge alien conspiracies. *Well, minus the whole part about having a son on another planet,* he thought. He also took small solace in the fact that he had known that his son would never have to hide the same secrets he did.

"Don't you have to pick up Liz?" Isabel asked, looking at her watch and making a face that implied his delayed departure was beginning to interfere with her plans for the day.

"On my way." He threw his bag onto his shoulder and headed for the door. "What are you up to this weekend?"

"Oh, nothing special," she replied, following him through the house. "Probably just hang out with Kyle and stuff." Of course, the "and stuff" she was referring to was Jesse. She was going to meet him for coffee that evening, but save their big plans until tomorrow. Considering that her whole family would be out of town, they would never have a better chance to spend a day together without fear of running into Max or her parents. Roswell was not a huge town to begin with, but it became even smaller when a simple dinner in a restaurant turned into a covert activity. Aside from that, however, she really did want to spend some time that day with Kyle to try to help him get over his problem without relying on alien manipulation.

"Have fun," Max said, opening the front door.

"You too," Isabel replied as she watched her brother leave. Then, she added in a mockingly stern voice, "You keep that kid in his place."

"I will." He cheerfully walked down the front path, actually looking forward to what lay ahead.

Hopping into his convertible and starting the ignition, Max was still getting used to how the car handled. The ride was a little more smooth than his old Jeep, although the gear shift did have a tendency to stick from time to time. As he drove the short distance from his place to the Crashdown, he thought once again of how much he missed the Jeep that he had owned since learning to drive.

When he, Isabel, Michael, and Tess had attempted to return to their home planet, they had set in motion a very specific plan for their disappearance from Roswell. The plot had involved a never delivered video message to his parents followed by the premature demise of his Jeep. Driving out to a deserted portion of road, Max flung the vehicle off the edge and into a valley using his powers to make it burst into flames along the way.

The ridding of the Jeep was quite spectacular and, unfortunately, quite irreversible. So, when Max later sent Tess packing and remained behind with his sister and Michael, he was forced to get a new ride and try to explain to his parents just what he had done with the old one. Just one more lie in an ever growing list.

Pulling up in the alley behind the Crashdown Café, Max was happy to find Liz waiting outside with her bag. Maria was also with her, obviously on break, since she was dressed in her work uniform. Initially, he had been planning to go the gentlemanly route and actually park his car and go inside to get Liz. However, that would have called for him to walk through the restaurant and possibly run into her father. Although Mr. Parker knew that Max was taking her to Artesia, Liz's dad also thought that it was just a drop-off-and-return trip. It was much easier for Max to ignore the fact that he was staying the weekend if he didn't actually have to lie to Mr. Parker's face.

"Have I ever mentioned how much I love a man in a convertible?" Maria cooed as she slid her hand along the now parked car.

"I thought you loved a man on a motorcycle," Liz replied, referring indirectly to Michael.

"Not at the moment," she answered in a huff.

Sill hoping to avoid getting involved in Michael and Maria's business, Max hopped out of the car to help Liz with her bag, giving her a quick peck on the cheek.

"My parents wanted you to come in so they could thank you for taking me to Artesia," Liz said, smiling warmly.

Max dropped the bag into the backseat as a look of horror crossed his face. "Really . . . that's . . . not . . ."

"I told them that we wanted to get on the road as soon as possible so we wouldn't be late," she quickly added, letting him off the hook.

"Don't want to have to deal with that crazy traffic between here and Artesia," Maria added sarcastically, since the road they were taking was never that busy, especially late on a Friday morning.

"Then maybe we should leave before they come out here to thank me?" Max suggested, with an eagerness in his tone.

Liz moved around the car toward the passenger side. "Maria, you've got the number in case anything happens while we're gone?"

"In my purse," she replied. "But what could possibly happen in this quiet little town?"

A flood of possibilities came to all three of their minds, but no one dared comment for risk of jinxing themselves.

"You two kids have fun," Maria quickly added. "And don't worry about us back here in Roswell. We'll be fine."

"Tell Michael I said good-bye," Max said, starting the car. "And remind him not to stop by my house."

"Yeah," she replied.

"Bye," Liz said as they drove off.

Maria watched them pull out into the street before heading back to work.

Making their way through Roswell, Max followed the familiar route to 285 South. The radio played softly, competing with the wind whipping past them in the convertible. The ride would take about an hour, but it would give them a chance to be alone in what seemed like the first time in a while.

"So, who exactly are we watching this weekend?" Max asked as they pulled onto the highway. "You never really explained who this kid is and how you know him."

"My friend Jason," Liz explained while putting on some sunscreen for the ride in the topless car. "He's about twelve now. Our moms were best friends in high school and got married around the same time. It was one of those things where I called his parents Aunt Jackie and Uncle Rob."

"Yeah, I have a set of those," Max commented.

"Jason was born when I was five," Liz continued as they headed down the highway. "Since we were both only children, we kind of fell into a big sister–little brother thing."

"Why is this the first time I've heard of him?" Max asked.

"We've been out of touch for over a year now," she explained, rubbing the lotion onto her arms. "His parents got divorced when he was six, and his dad wound up moving to New York to take a job. About a year later, Aunt Jackie met a man from Artesia named George Lyles."

"Uncle George?" Max anticipated where this was going.

"Well, no," she corrected him. "I never really got to know him, since he lived down in Artesia. I mean, our families did spend some time together. I was even flower girl at their wedding. But I never really felt close enough to call him uncle. I usually call him Mr. Lyles."

"So after the wedding, Aunt Jackie and Jason moved to Artesia?" Max asked.

"A little over four years ago"—she motioned to offer him the suntan lotion, but he shook his head to decline— "we would drive down there or they would come up to Roswell about once a month. Then the trips started getting less frequent. Mr. Lyles rarely joined us since his ranch kept him so busy."

"Ranch?" Max asked while pulling aside to let a tailgater pass as the guy was intent on going thirty miles over the speed limit.

"They raise sheep," Liz continued. "Cute, huh? They only have a few. Mr. Lyles inherited the ranch from his parents. He's actually some kind of important businessman who telecommutes and flies to Dallas once a month. His parents died long ago, and he moved onto the property and kept the sheep. Which means there will probably be a ranch hand or two around this weekend, but they probably won't come near the house."

"Good to know," he said, making a mental note to stay away from wherever the sheep were kept, so no one found out he had stayed the weekend.

"Eventually, the trips stopped entirely," Liz said. "But Jason and I kept in touch with letters, phone calls, and eventually e-mails. Then, over a year ago, he stopped writing at all. I would send him little updates of what was going on in my life, glossing over any otherworldly happenings, of course, but he never responded."

"I guess you were surprised when your parents asked you to take care of him for the weekend?"

"Well, Mom and Aunt Jackie kept in touch," Liz said.

"But, yeah, it was a little out of the blue. Mom kind of implied that Jason's been having some . . . well, she wouldn't exactly *say* trouble, but something's going on. I guess Aunt Jackie thought he might like to see a friend."

Max felt another pang of guilt about tagging along on the weekend sojourn. "Are you sure I won't be getting in the way? I can just drop you off, turn around, and go home like your parents already think I'm doing."

"You're not getting out of this so easily," Liz said, smiling at his reluctance. "You wanted to know what it was like taking care of a child. Well, here you have a child for the weekend. I'm sure nothing's seriously wrong with Jason. Besides, he's going to love meeting you."

"If you say so," Max said, although he was beginning to have a sense of foreboding about the coming weekend.

The pair drove along, enjoying the beautiful weather and shifting their conversation to the subject of absolutely nothing important for a while. Max couldn't help but enjoy spending time with Liz when there was no alien threat or their occasionally overbearing parents for the foreseeable future. He actually laughed out loud several times, which he knew he had not done for a long, long time, as they talked about their plans for senior year of high school and regular teenage stuff. But, before too long their ride was coming near the end as they passed a sign welcoming them to Artesia.

"The Lyleses' ranch is on the other side of town," Liz explained as they drove past a huge oil refinery and into the city proper. "Just keep driving along this road and we'll come to a turnoff."

"Gotcha," he replied.

"I forgot what a nice town this is," Liz said, admiring the view. "Have you ever been here before?"

"Just driving through," Max replied. "Never stopped."

"The town is named after the artesian wells that were discovered in 1903," she explained. "The town thrives on its cattle and sheep ranches and its alfalfa, cotton, chili, and pecan farming."

"What? Did you memorize a tour guide?" Max smiled at her wealth of information. "Can you quote me facts on population and climate?"

"Population is around twelve thousand residents," Liz answered. "The climate is dry, with around twelve inches of rain annually."

Taking his eyes off the road for a second, Max looked at his girlfriend, both frightened and impressed by her geek-like knowledge of the town.

"When Jason moved here, I helped him pull together all this information so he wouldn't be so afraid to leave Roswell for some unknown place," she explained. "He insisted that I keep a copy of it too so I would always remember where he lives. I found it this morning when I was going through some stuff."

"And here I was just thinking that you were showing off how smart you are," Max said, giving her a pat on the leg.

"I was." Liz giggled. "There is one other interesting piece of information. In nineteen eighty-nine, the Federal Law Enforcement Training Center opened here to educate people from all over the world in specialized law enforcement practices."

Max felt a rock in the pit of his stomach. "Funny how you failed to mention that part until we got here."

"Come on, Max." Liz got serious for a moment. "There's absolutely nothing to worry about. We're just having a normal weekend of baby-sitting."

Famous last words, he thought.

Liz pointed out the turnoff, and Max followed her directions, eventually pulling his convertible into the looping driveway of a beautiful, large, ranch-style house. Admiring the property, he parked directly behind a high-priced, limited edition Land Rover. The back door was open, and a few overnight bags were already inside. Obviously, Mr. and Mrs. Lyles were readying the car for their trip.

"You're here," a man's voice said from the house as soon as Max turned the engine off. "Good, we'll be able to get on the road right away."

"Hello, Mr. Lyles," Liz said as she got out of the car.

Max immediately noticed that her voice had fallen into a tone she usually reserved for teachers and law enforcement agents. He watched as Mr. Lyles gave a nod of hello and proceeded to put another duffel bag into the SUV, shifting the bags so they were nicely organized. Max couldn't help but think that the man was just stalling so he wouldn't have to come over to say hello.

"Liz!" a voice excitedly shouted from the house.

Max turned to see a woman about his own mother's age come running out of the house and embrace Liz in the type of hug usually reserved for close family members.

"Aunt Jackie." Liz's voice immediately returned to the warm tone that Max knew and loved. "It's so good to see you."

"And who is this fine young man?" she asked as they

broke their embrace. Max was getting out of the car, and the sudden attention made him blush.

"This is Max," Liz began the introduction. "He drove—"

"Yes, I've heard all about you, you little heartbreaker," she said in a friendly, nonthreatening tone as she made her way around the car to give him a hug. "George, come here and say hi."

In response, Mr. Lyles nodded hello as he slammed the rear door closed on the SUV. "We should get going, Jackie. It's a long trip to Santa Fe."

"Santa Fe?" Max asked with immediate interest. "Is that where you're going?"

"They have this great arts festival," Jackie said, still holding on to Max's hand.

"I know," Max said, and couldn't help but smile along with the contagiously happy woman. "My parents are going down tomorrow. They go every year."

"Well, I finally convinced George to take me," she said with a smile, although it was obvious to Max by the look on Mr. Lyles's face that she hadn't succeeded in convincing him that he'd have a good time.

"It's getting late," Mr. Lyles said, consulting his watch.

"Oh, I thought we were early," Liz said.

"You are," Jackie said, shooting her husband a glance but never losing her smile for a moment. "It's just that no one's ever early enough for him."

"Max, it was nice meeting you," Mr. Lyles said, still standing a short distance away by his SUV. "Liz," he said, and nodded to her. Then he got into the car and started the engine.

Aunt Jackie's smile faltered for an almost imperceptible

moment when she heard the engine revving. "Jason's in his room," she said as she started back around the car to give Liz another hug. "Sorry we have to leave so quickly. Max, it was nice meeting you. I'll see you Sunday when you come to pick up Liz."

Max watched as she hurried into the SUV. As soon as the door was closed, Mr. Lyles was pulling away.

"Well, that was easy," Max said as he came around the car to join Liz.

"For once," she added.

Max and Liz entered the house through the still open front door. The place was larger than they were used to, with an actual second floor, which none of their friends had in their respective homes and apartments. Max marveled at the size of the place, and the expensive-looking furniture all in pristine condition. This was especially notable since there was a preteen living in the place.

Something else he couldn't help but notice was the pure whiteness of it all. Stepping into the living room, he immediately fixated on the fluffy white couch and matching chair, as well as the bright white paint on the walls and the sheer white curtains. He felt like he should take a shower and change his clothes before he sat down on anything.

"Clean, huh?" Liz asked, reading his mind.

"Are you sure a kid lives here?" he asked.

"It took a while for me to get used to it too," Liz replied, looking around. "Jason must not know I'm here yet," she said, attempting to explain the absence of her young friend.

"Don't you think it's strange how his parents didn't say

good-bye before they left?" Max asked, following.

"They must have said it before," she replied. "Aunt Jackie wouldn't have gone anywhere without making sure Jason was okay first. Wait till you meet him. He's the sweetest kid you'll ever know." She started up the stairs to where she remembered his room to be. "I'll be right back."

While Liz was upstairs getting her friend, Max continued his tour of the first floor. From the living room, he peered into an office. It wasn't as bright white as the room he had come from, but was pristine nonetheless. He assumed this was where Mr. Lyles did his telecommuting.

Continuing the tour, he walked through the dining room and into the kitchen, finding each room to be even cleaner than the last. The chrome accents in the kitchen actually glistened because they were so sparkling clean. The stovetop looked as if it had never been used, and so did the microwave, which he confirmed by opening the door and looking inside. Dinner was still hours away and he was already worried about spilling food.

His self-guided tour eventually led him back to the living room, where he realized that it was taking Liz an awfully long time to return with Jason. Assuming they were just catching up, he gave them a few more minutes before finally deciding to see what was going on. Making his way up the stairs, he followed the voice of his girlfriend and found her pleading with a closed door.

"Come on, Jason," Liz said to the door. "Let me in."

Silence.

"Problem?" Max asked as he joined her.

"Jason won't open the door," she looked to Max, who took his own turn knocking on the door without a response. Again, Max had that same sense of foreboding he'd had earlier.

"Jason," he said. "This is Liz's friend, Max. Is anything wrong?"

Silence.

This is not going to be a fun weekend, Max thought with a sigh.

4

Kyle's eyes were drooping slowly as he sat on the couch watching some of the most painful daytime television he had ever seen. Another night with only a few hours of restless sleep left him so tired and dragging that he actually didn't mind sitting through the cheating spouses threatening to throw chairs at each other on the ridiculous talk show with the lame host. *Well, my life could always be worse,* he thought. *I could be one of those people.*

His boss at the shop had noticed his lackluster performance over the past few days and had figured that a sleepy worker in an auto shop was a dangerous combination, so he had told Kyle to take a long weekend off. Almost an entire day still ahead of him, Kyle knew that he should try to get some extra sleep, but every time his eyelids met each other, the same thing would happen.

Flash.

Alex falling to the ground in Kyle's bedroom.

Flash.

Alex, lying bloody in his wrecked car.

Flash.

Kyle sitting alone in his room. The door locked.

Knocking.

In his dream *and* in his ears as well. Kyle's eyes shot open as he thought he heard his name being called by a familiar and friendly voice. Back in the realm of the living, Kyle realized that someone was at the door. "Come in!" he yelled without moving from the couch.

"It's about time," Isabel said as she showed herself into his house. "I've been standing out there for a minute. . . . You look like crap."

"Funny how you're not the first person to have mentioned that to me lately," Kyle said, trying not to be offended. She had spoken the truth. "What do you want?"

"Maybe we should try this again," Isabel said, referring to their less than stellar greetings. "Good morning, Kyle, what's new?"

"Good morning, Isabel." He tried to match her revised mood, but failed miserably. "Absolutely nothing is new since the other night."

"That's why I'm here," Isabel said.

"You've changed your mind." His body finally perked up as he sat up straight on the couch. "You're going to dreamwalk me? End the nightmares?"

"No, Kyle," she said gently, sitting beside him. "But I thought we could spend the afternoon together. Maybe take your mind off your troubles, as they say."

He tried not to look too disappointed. After all, she did care about him, and was only doing what she thought best. But once again he failed miserably as his body slumped back into the couch.

"Isabel, it's been about two months since I remembered Alex's death," he reminded her. "We've been through the trauma of Max's child and your canceled departure—to say nothing of final exams. Somehow, I don't think one afternoon is going to do it."

"That's because you don't know what I have in store for you." She stood with a gleam in her eye. "Come on, what have you got to lose?"

Since Kyle couldn't argue with that logic, he finally got up off the couch. Grabbing the remote, he put an end to the torturous screams of the woman dressed entirely in Lycra on the television. *Now I'll never know if she forgives her two-timing husband.* He smirked. *Darn.*

"I walked over here," Isabel explained as they left the house, "so we're going to need to take your car."

Kyle reached into his pocket and pulled out the keys, handing them to Isabel. "You'd better drive. My reflex time is a little slow this morning."

"Mind if I put the top down?" she asked as they got into the red convertible.

"Why not?" he went along.

Isabel started the engine, and Kyle indicated the button that she would need to push. His convertible was one of the best parts of living in Roswell. Being in a desert meant that he rarely needed to drive around with the top up to protect him from rain—which he figured probably also explained why Max kept getting vehicles without roofs as well.

Kyle continued to fight against sleep as Isabel drove his car through the streets of Roswell, talking about her mysterious fun plans for the afternoon. The smooth rolling of the car was lulling him as he listened to his friend.

Flash.

The vultures were circling overhead.

His eyes popped open once again as Kyle woke from his daytime nightmare. He looked over to see if Isabel had noticed, but she was still going on about how much fun they were going to have. In actuality, Kyle felt that whenever people talked about the amount of fun they *were going* to have, it probably meant they weren't going to enjoy themselves at all. However, for Isabel's sake, he decided to keep an open mind. Anything would be better than a day of bad television and nightmare flashes.

"Here we are!" Isabel pulled him out of his musings.

"The Crashdown?" Kyle said as the car pulled into an empty spot beside their favorite hangout. "That's your big plan?"

"For starters," she replied as they got out of the car. "Trust me."

Walking in the door of the restaurant, it was immediately clear they had come in during the lunch rush. Summer was always a little more hectic in there, since it was the tourist season and the theme restaurant really catered to the specific tastes of most out-of-town visitors. Conveniently, Isabel saw a pair of tourists getting out of a booth, and hurried Kyle over to it. "I thought Michael and Maria might want to join us after their shift is over."

As they sat at the still messy table, Maria hurried over with a bus tray to clear away the plates. Isabel did not envy her for spending the summer clearing dishes and serving the bustling summer tourist trade. Then again, Isabel remembered that she needed to start thinking about possibly getting her own job soon. After graduating early from high school, she had spent some time helping out in her dad's law office, but that had gotten complicated when she started seeing Jesse. Since Isabel wasn't really interested in law, she recently thanked her dad for the opportunity, but told him that she was going to pursue other employment. Unfortunately she hadn't had the time to do any serious job searching, and it looked like she was going to have to put it off a little while longer. There was cheering up to be done.

"Hey, Maria, what are you and Michael up to this afternoon?" Isabel innocently asked.

Suddenly, the plates that had been gently placed in the tray were now being slammed together. "I don't know what *he's* planning to do, but I'm thinking of coloring my hair. How do you think I'd look if I dyed it black?"

"Awful," Kyle said abruptly and honestly.

Maria didn't seem the least bit offended, which suggested to Isabel that their friend was considering making that particular change purely for the shock value. Of course, that translated into the fact that Maria and Michael were obviously still fighting. *When is Maria ever going to learn that Michael notices her even if she doesn't do crazy things?*

"If you'd like to see," Isabel suggested conspiratorially, "I can do it for you with no lasting effects."

"That's okay," Maria said as she wiped down the table. "It was only an idea."

"So do you want to join us?" Isabel asked.

"I wish I could," Maria said, "but my mom's been on me to help her catalog her new alien autopsy artifacts. Sorry."

The apology was obviously directed to her inability to join them as well as to the way she'd be spending her day.

Isabel always felt strange around Maria's mom. She liked the woman well enough, but couldn't get over the fact that Ms. DeLuca was profiting off jokes based on the single biggest tragedy of Isabel's life. *Then again, so is ninety percent of the town of Roswell,* she thought as she surveyed the patrons of the Crashdown eating their alien-themed meals.

"Do you guys want anything to drink?" Maria asked as she balanced the bus tray on her hip.

"A Rocket Root Beer Float," Isabel said, figuring today was the kind of day to ignore calories and pig out. Comfort food always worked for her, so she figured that it could easily help Kyle as well.

Kyle just nodded as if to say, "Make it two."

Isabel could tell that Maria was about to make a comment but apparently had thought better of it. Instead, she turned with the tray and went back behind the counter to make the drinks. Isabel then focused her attention on Kyle, who looked rather pitiful slumped down on his side of the booth.

A long, very uncomfortable pause ensued.

Kyle's fingers drummed on the table.

Tap, tap, tap. Tap, tap.

"I'll go check with Michael," she said, getting up from the booth.

As Isabel walked across the restaurant she silently hoped that Michael would be up for their little afternoon adventure. Kyle's miserable attitude was beginning to make the task of cheering him up seem impossible, so she thought that bringing another person along could help her effort. Of course, Michael wasn't exactly the first person who came to mind when the task involved having a positive attitude.

Reaching the large service window, Isabel leaned into the kitchen to find her friend in his usual position flipping burgers on the grill. "Hey, Michael!"

"What do you want?" he said in a surly tone as he dropped a basket of fries into the boiling grease, keeping his back to her as he concentrated on food preparation.

"Never mind." She spun around and headed back for the table. *One miserable person is enough for the day.*

"That was fast." Kyle seemed to be slumped even lower when she returned.

"Michael wasn't exactly in the kind of mood I was looking for," Isabel replied. "Then again, he never really is."

Was that a slight smile on Kyle's face?

Maria returned to the table with their drinks and to take their lunch order. She seemed only mildly happier than Michael, although as a waitress her job was to be perky as to ensure the better tip, so she just grinned her way through whatever the problem was this time. Isabel never bothered to ask about their situation, because she knew that it would work itself out eventually. It always did.

Once the order was placed, their food came much faster than usual, which Isabel attributed to the fact that the cook and waitress weren't engaging in idle chitchat to keep them from their jobs. As she sat in the booth with Kyle, she managed to coax him into a conversation about his new job as a mechanic. The goal of the talk and the entire afternoon was to avoid anything even remotely alien in nature—a challenge, to say the least, in Roswell, the alien capital of the world.

After lunch, Isabel started their fun-time tour at the Museum of Contemporary Arts. Even though she knew this kind of entertainment was not Kyle's speed, it had the desired effect when he started making many jokes about the collection of modern art and, more specifically, the modern artists. One particular painting of a black line that had a plaque beneath it claiming its value was several thousand dollars nearly had him in hysterics. Isabel decided that she would come back to the museum Saturday with Jesse so they could seriously enjoy the works.

Following the museum, Isabel took him to the Spring River Park. It had been years since she had played on the playground, and figured that the same was true for Kyle. She couldn't exactly picture Kyle and his football buddies hanging out in a place where the average patron was about four years old, not counting their mothers and the rogue father every now and then. The trip was entirely worth it just to see Kyle trying to fit onto one of the kiddie swings. She took it as a good sign when Kyle laughed out loud after a little girl stole a swing right out from under him, sticking out her tongue as if she owned the playground equipment.

They capped off their time at the park with a ride on the carousel. Again, this was something neither she nor Kyle had done in years. They both commented on how huge the merry-go-round had seemed to them as children, but now the Roswell carousel appeared really rather limited compared with those huge wooden ones they had seen in movies. But that didn't matter as they continued to ride round and round for almost a half hour.

When they were finally kicked off the ride, Isabel took Kyle on a stroll through the zoo that was attached to the park. The last time either of them had been there was during a seventh-grade field trip, but the place hadn't changed all that much since then. In fact, they even remembered some of the animals from the field trip. All in all, they were both having a good day.

Leaving the park, they walked back into town to retrieve Kyle's car, which they had left at the Crashdown because the weather was nice enough for them to get everywhere on foot without suffering from heat exhaustion typical to most Roswell summers. Most of their stroll was spent in animated conversation as they went over all the fun details of their day.

"Thanks, Isabel." Kyle openly beamed like a man without a care in the world. "I'm having a great time."

Isabel silently patted herself on the back as she tried to discreetly look at her watch. "I knew you would."

"So what's next?" he innocently asked as they walked down the streets of Roswell.

The unspoken response was *coffee with Jesse*, but Isabel couldn't say that because of her decision to keep the relationship on the sly. Even though she had been enjoying their conversation, she had also spent the past fifteen minutes trying to figure out a way to extricate herself from their activities for her secret rendezvous without spoiling Kyle's mood. The day's activities were supposed to have taken Kyle's mind off his problems *and* make him tired enough for a full night of sleep. But he seemed more awake than when she had picked him up earlier, and was ready to stay out and have fun.

And she was already five minutes late.

"I promised to have dinner with my parents," she lied. "Since they're going to Santa Fe tomorrow."

"Oh." The look of disappointment on Kyle's face nearly made her cancel her plans on the spot. She noticed that he had absentmindedly started drumming the fingers of his right hand against his leg. He hadn't done that since the museum.

"But maybe we can get together afterward," she immediately suggested since she knew Jesse had plans to go out with one of his friends later. "Maybe we could just hang out at your place?"

"Okay." Kyle didn't really sound thrilled to be left alone even for a short time.

It seemed to Isabel that all the work she had done over the past few hours had served absolutely no purpose at all, since Kyle was suddenly back in the same mood that he had greeted her with earlier in the day. Then she noticed that his expression changed yet again. His face was totally blank as he stared at the traffic in the street.

"Kyle?" Her eyes followed his gaze, and she saw a dark-colored car turning onto the main drag. At first she thought it looked a little like Alex's car, but it was a totally different make and model. However, in the fading light of sunset, the color did appear close enough for her to make the false assumption.

Looking back to Kyle, she watched as his eyes tracked the car while it drove down the street. At first, an almost imperceptible shudder ran through his body. But, soon enough, he was shaking violently.

"Kyle?" she called to him, but it was like he was miles

away. His eyes seemed to be pleading with the driver to stop, and his body looked like it was about to spring into action and run after the phantom car. His fingers tapped wildly against his own body. "Kyle, you're scaring me!"

But he continued to ignore her as the voices ran through his mind.

Tap, tap, tap. Tap, tap.

Slowly, the car made another turn off the street and out of their line of sight. Isabel actually watched Kyle's body make a physical change as he regained his composure. He was breathing heavily as a drop of perspiration rolled down his forehead. He finally blinked.

"Are you okay?" she asked.

"Yeah," he said in a hollow voice.

"That was no daydream," she said.

"I know," he replied. "I get kind of thrown into them whenever something even remotely reminds me of Alex or Tess."

"Are they always that bad?" she asked.

"That was mild," he said without a trace of sarcasm.

Suddenly Isabel knew that her plans with Jesse were about to be cancelled. As luck would have it, they were already back at the Crashdown Café. "Kyle, would you mind waiting in here for a few minutes? I have to run a quick errand."

"Sure," he said. "I could use a milk shake anyway."

Isabel remembered how much milk shakes had seemed to be a cure-all for every dark situation when she was a child. Going back to the original theme of good fun and comfort food, she felt the need for a shake herself. "Order me one too. I'll be right back."

As soon as Kyle went inside the restaurant, Isabel was off down the street. Conveniently, the coffeehouse where she was to meet Jesse was only a few blocks away. Since Roswell wasn't a huge bustling metropolis, they only had a coffeehouse every fourth block instead of every other block as in most major cities.

Seeing the sign for Bean There, Done That, Isabel slowed herself and grabbed the compact from her small pocketbook to do a quick makeup check. She was still in the early stages of her relationship with Jesse and she didn't want him to see her without so much as a hair out of place. After a quick lipstick reapply, she opened the door into the overly air-conditioned coffeehouse. With a shiver, she stepped inside.

Isabel found Jesse immediately, which wasn't difficult because the place only had four small tables—two of which were empty. He had been kind enough to wait for her without ordering, which Isabel couldn't help but notice obviously annoyed the guy behind the counter since Jesse was taking up a seat without having purchased a beverage.

It's a coffeehouse, she thought. *People are supposed to loiter.*

A perfect gentleman, Jesse was up and pulling out the seat for Isabel before she even reached the table. He gave her a hug with a quick kiss hello as she arrived, and waited for her to take her seat before sitting himself.

She chose to remain standing. "I'm sorry I'm late," she said.

"You're worth the wait," he replied, indicating that she should sit down.

"I hope you still think so when I have to cancel on you," she said with a flirtatious and apologetic smile.

"But you're already here," he said.

The guy at the counter was looking at them expectantly. It was as if they were taking up major table space in the practically empty coffeehouse.

"Would you believe I have to take care of a sick friend?" she asked. "A *really* sick friend," she added, leaving out the fact that Kyle's illness was more mental than physical.

"Is it serious?" he asked, and she gave him extra points for the fact that he was obviously concerned.

"We don't know," she replied.

"Well, then, you should stay with her," Jesse said, starting to walk her to the door. "We're still on for tomorrow, right?"

"Of course," Isabel replied without correcting the assumed gender of her friend. "Thanks for understanding."

The guy behind the counter looked rather annoyed as they stepped out of the establishment and back onto the sidewalk. Isabel couldn't help but notice how Jesse had let the door slam behind him, assuming it was done on purpose to let the coffee guy know he hadn't liked being stalked while waiting for his date.

"Until tomorrow," he said, giving her a more serious kiss on the lips. "And remember, you're all mine for the entire day."

Reluctantly, Isabel broke from his embrace and started to make her way back to the Crashdown, peering over her shoulder every few seconds to keep him in her sight as long as possible. Even though she knew that Kyle needed her, she couldn't help but feel guilty over the fact that she had to blow off Jesse to be there for her friend, especially considering how understanding Jesse had been about everything.

Once Jesse was finally out of sight, she replayed their conversation in her head and was confused about why she hadn't corrected him and explained that her friend was male. Certainly Jesse would have understood that a sick friend was a sick friend no matter what gender. She just chalked it up to the growing ease at which she had taken to lying about things after having had so much practice. It was not necessarily one of her better personality traits.

One day, she promised herself, *I'm going to tell Jesse everything.*

5

"**B**aby-sitting is much easier than I thought it would be." Max was comfortably leaning back into the Lyleses' plush white leather couch, careful to keep his sock-clad feet off the glass coffee table. "Especially considering that we haven't seen Jason since we got here."

They had been in the Lyleses' home for well over five hours and hadn't even seen their charge. Every now and again, they thought they heard footsteps above them, but whenever either of them called upstairs, they got no response. At least a toilet had flushed once letting them know that Jason was still alive up there.

"He's got to come down for dinner," Liz said as she looked through the take-out menus Aunt Jackie had left on the kitchen counter for her. "How about pizza?"

"Sounds good to me," Max said, distracted by the silence from the second floor.

"Should we see what Jason wants on it?" Liz asked as she pulled the menu for the pizza parlor out of the pile.

"I think we've played his game long enough." Max got

up from the couch with a determined look on his face. "Order whatever you want. I'll be down with Jason in a minute."

Liz watched as Max went upstairs, looking more focused than she had ever seen him—and she had seen him in many intense situations. "First lesson in fatherhood coming up," she said softly to herself.

Outside Jason's bedroom door, Max took a deep breath and prepared himself for whatever it was that was about to happen.

"Jason, this is Liz's friend, Max," he reintroduced himself through the closed door as he banged on it. "We're ordering dinner. Open up."

"Go to Hell!" the kid yelled back.

Not a great start, Max thought. *On the bright side, he finally spoke.*

"Look, Jason." Max decided to take the gentle route. "We haven't even met, and I certainly don't know what's going on, but I'm sure Liz and I have nothing to do with it. Why don't you open the door and we can talk about it?"

Silence.

Okay, new direction.

Max placed his hand over the lock. "Jason, if you don't open this door, I'm coming in."

"Go ahead," Jason yelled. "It's locked—hey, how'd you do that?" he asked as the door opened.

"A little trick of the baby-sitting trade," Max said cryptically from the now open doorway. "Come downstairs and I might consider showing you some other tricks."

Intrigued, and lacking any other option, Jason got up and stormed out of the room.

Max followed as the twelve-year-old made his way downstairs. Jason seemed somewhat tall for his age and rather pale considering he lived in a desert. He had a shock of black hair that Max figured must have come from his father, since his mother's hair was light brown. *Although she could have had it colored,* he supposed.

Jason's clothes matched his hair, as he was outfitted in black from head to toe in a T-shirt and jeans that had obviously been bought for him when he was a few pounds heavier, since the clothes hung rather loosely on his body. Max knew from past experience what a crazy time period this was in a boy's life, and attributed the almost intensely skinny body to changes that Jason was probably undergoing. He was an attractive kid, and Max thought that once Jason's body got through this tumultuous period he would probably have a number of girls interested in him.

Liz came out from the living room when she heard footsteps plodding down the stairs. She tried to keep her excitement in check, considering how rude he had been to ignore her for so long. "Jason, it's good to finally see you."

"What's for dinner?" was his short response.

"We haven't seen each other in over two years and all you have to say is, 'What's for dinner?'" Liz was visibly hurt by the boy's abrupt manner.

Max noticed that Jason seemed to be sorry for his rudeness, but only for a moment. The stone face of resolve quickly went back up as he chose to remain silent. Max figured he was like most preteens and was probably just angry at the world for no particular reason. Since he hadn't even truly met the boy, he wasn't going to take any of it personally, but he wished he could say the same for

Liz, who appeared to be more than a little hurt by her young friend's attitude.

"We're getting pizza," Max spoke as abruptly as Jason had, then took Liz by the arm to guide her back into the living room.

"What are we doing?" she whispered.

"Ignoring him," Max replied, also in a whisper. "Don't worry, he'll follow."

Then they heard the front door slam shut.

"Time for a new plan," Liz said as she hurried back into the hall and flung the door open. "Jason, freeze!"

He had only gotten a few steps away from the house when Liz's voice stopped him cold. With shoulders slumped, his back was still to her, but she had definitely gotten his attention.

Max came up behind her to watch what she was doing and provide backup if necessary. But her body language told him that, for the moment, his assistance was not required.

"In the house," she said in one of the most firm tones of voice Max had ever heard her use, "now!"

"You don't have to talk to me like I'm a baby," Jason moped as he came back into his home.

"Then stop acting like one," Liz replied, shutting the door behind them.

Jason sulked into the living room and deposited himself on the couch. Max and Liz followed and took seats on either side of the boy. They sat in total silence until the pizza came.

Max paid the delivery guy while Liz brought the pizza into the dining room. They had wanted to just relax and eat while watching TV, but one look at the pristine living room convinced them that sitting at a table would be their best option. So, instead of the random noises of whatever was on the tube, the three of them settled in for a very quiet dinner.

Forty miles away in Michael's apartment, another dinner was taking place with an even greater amount of hostile silence. A meal carried out with equal amounts of anger and absolute quiet was in itself an art form, one at which Maria and Michael had become masters.

It had started when Michael had placed on his plate the piece of lemon chicken that Maria had prepared. A scrape of the fork against the ceramic dish evoked a dirty look from Maria as she assumed it had been an intentional message aimed at her. She answered with an abrupt clink of her own fork onto her plate, clearly indicating that he should have let her serve herself first considering that she was not only the cook but the only lady present and it was the gentlemanly thing to do. Michael only glanced up briefly as he continued to ignore her.

The meal progressed to the next phase with the passing of side dishes. First, Maria took a small helping of her world-famous string bean casserole and placed the bowl down on Michael's side of the table, but not into his waiting hands. She made sure it landed with a definite thud. Michael countered by taking a heaping spoonful and plopping the casserole onto his plate, spilling some of it onto the table. Maria rolled her eyes at his gluttony.

Then came the passing of the rolls. Both participants reached to the center of the table for the bread at the same time, grabbing their own pieces while their hands momentarily grazed each other. There was a bit of hesitation as they looked into each other's eyes and knew that they were both tempted to take their rolls and use them as projectiles to be launched at each other. However, the possibility of a harmlessly flirtatious food fight was the furthest thing from their minds as they considered the hot buttered weapons.

"You didn't have to come if you were going to be in a mood." Michael slammed his roll onto his plate to punctuate his statement.

"Oh, no." Maria tore into her own roll with a viciousness rarely seen outside of the jungle. "I promised a week ago to make you dinner. I don't want it to look like I don't honor my commitments."

"Are you trying to make some kind of point?" he asked.

Maria couldn't help but think that her boyfriend was clueless. "Nope. No point at all. I'm just sitting here having a wonderfully prepared meal."

More hostile silence as they continued to eat.

Progressing beyond the scraping of forks, Michael took their conflict to the next level by chewing with his mouth open, although the action was most likely unintentional. Even so, Maria shot him a look of disgust before pointing her fork toward his mouth in a threatening manner. Understanding her meaning, Michael closed his mouth, taking each bite with precise care.

"Why couldn't you do anything at Alex's memorial?" Maria asked suddenly, cutting into the silent meal.

Michael swallowed the piece of chicken he was chewing with his mouth closed. "I cooked."

"And a meal prepared by you is always a creative endeavor." Maria shifted the food around on her plate. "Why couldn't you perform something?"

"What? Sing along with the band?" he replied sarcastically. "Are you insane?"

"Obviously," she said, taking a bite of her roll, contemplating her response as she chewed. "You could have done the skit with Max and Isabel."

"I'm not a comedian," he replied.

"You're telling me."

More silence.

Food was being pushed around on both plates as Michael and Maria apparently gave up on the meal altogether.

"What is it with this quiet loner routine?" Maria asked.

"What routine?" he said. "It's who I am. Sorry if I can't do tricks for you. I'm not a trained dog."

"Pity," she replied.

"And what's with you?" He changed his position from defense to offense. "Why can't you just accept me for who I am and stop trying to change me?"

"Gee, I wonder," she replied sarcastically.

"You always have to be so condescending!" he said.

The meal had been forgotten, and the hostile silence had evolved into hostile debate.

"Because you're always so impossible," she shot back, standing up. "I don't know why I even came here."

"Finally, something we agree on." He rose so quickly that his chair fell behind him.

"Oh no, don't get up," she said, although he was already standing. "No need to develop manners now. I can see myself out."

"Fine," he said, righting his chair to sit back down.

She looked at him like she was surprised he actually wasn't going to show her to the door. "Good-bye!"

"See ya," he replied from the chair.

Maria slammed the door shut behind her, pausing outside to take a few deep breaths. Unscrewing her bottle of relaxing cedar oil, she spilled a few drops under her tongue.

On the other side of the door, Michael was also huffing intensely, trying to calm himself. He looked at the remains of the partially uneaten meals on the table before setting his eyes on his kitchen counter, where he saw the chocolate cream pie that Maria had left behind.

Suddenly, his door swung open again as Maria came storming back inside.

"I forgot the dessert." She grabbed the pie from the counter and made her way back to the door.

Michael considered stopping her, if only to get back the pie, but he stayed in the chair. The door slammed even louder the second time she left. Waiting, Michael eventually accepted the fact that she was not going to return again.

Finally getting off the chair, Michael contemplated clearing the dishes, but put them off for the moment as his thoughts were elsewhere. Making his way across the room, he opened the closet, throwing assorted items out onto the floor as he reached along the back wall. Settling his hands on the large object he had been searching for, he pulled it out, careful not to let the cover slip off. He had been so cautious when he had put the item safely away weeks ago that he didn't want to do any damage to it now since he finally felt ready to see it once again.

* * *

Kyle slid the Men in Blackberry Pie to the middle of the table so they could share.

Isabel slid it right back in front of him. "I think I've had more than enough junk food today," she said, although she was staring longingly at the dessert.

"There's no such thing as too much junk food," he replied through a mouthful of the pie.

"Root beer floats at lunch, candy apples at the zoo, milk shakes before dinner," she said, listing just some of the snacking they had done during their day out, making a mental note to ask Jesse to spend some of their Saturday together walking around the entire perimeter of Roswell. "How can you still be eating?"

"Football season's just around the corner." He tore another piece of the pie away with his fork. "I've got to bulk up."

Oh, to be a guy, she thought. Then, she finally gave in and reached across the table to take a bite of her own. "We've been avoiding what happened outside."

"I'm glad your parents didn't mind you missing dinner with them," he said, deflecting her comment.

Isabel's thoughts flashed back to Jesse for a moment, since he was really the one she'd cancelled on. "And you're still avoiding the subject."

"What do you want me to say?" he asked, picking the remains of the pie apart with his fork. "I've had a great time today, but did you really think that one afternoon full of activities was going to erase those horrible images from my mind?"

"I was hoping to at least distract you for a while," she answered softly.

"And you did," he honestly replied. "But you know there's only one way to get rid of them for good."

"No, Kyle," she said firmly. "I can't dreamwalk you to remove the memories. It's too dangerous."

"More dangerous than my meltdown outside?" His fingers were tapping on the plate again, every now and again dropping into the pie. "What if that happens while I'm driving?"

"We should talk to Max about it when he gets back," Isabel said. "Maybe he'll have an idea."

"And until then I should just stay at home locked in my room?" Kyle asked. "I've already been told to take time off from work," he reminded her. "This is beginning to interfere with my life."

Isabel didn't want to fight with him, especially considering the agitated state he was already in. She tried to keep herself calm, even though he was getting a little unsettled. "I wish I had the answers, Kyle, but I don't."

"Yes, you do," he pushed.

Their eyes locked as Kyle pleaded with her to do what she knew she could not. She had already lost one friend to alien mind games; she was not going to lose another.

Finally, Kyle relented. His body sank back into the booth. "I'm sorry. I know it's dangerous. I'm just under a lot of stress."

"I know," she replied. "And I want to help, but I'm just afraid."

"Do you want the last bite?" He referred to the pie, although the remnants had been mashed into oblivion.

"I think you managed to put it out of its misery," she replied.

"Lucky pie," he joked.

"Come on, Kyle." She got out of the booth. "The night is still young. To paraphrase the poem Liz read the other night, we've got miles to go before you sleep." She put her hand out to him in friendship.

Rejuvenated, Kyle slid out from the booth and took her hand.

Isabel led him through the Crashdown and out into the street. The night ahead of them, she was determined to do whatever she could to keep his mind off his problems. All the while, she was beginning to question her decision not to dreamwalk him as the phrase kept repeating in her head, *miles to go before you sleep*.

6

As both meals came to very different conclusions in Roswell, another dinner came to an end forty miles south in Artesia. Max finally was able to relax once all the pizza had been eaten, considering he had spent most of the meal worrying that they were going to spill something on the perfectly clean beige carpet. A few times, he suspected that Jason had been aware of his concern, since the boy kept holding his glass of soda precariously over the floor with an evil grin on his face.

Having spent a little time with Jason, Max had to wonder whether this was the same person Liz had grown up with. He didn't seem at all like the boy she had described. *Talk about invasion of the body snatchers,* he thought. Then, for one infinitesimally brief moment he feared that was the truth behind Jason's behavior. *Stranger things have happened.* Shaking off the ridiculous thought, Max got up to clear away their mess.

After removing the remains of the slightly overcooked pizza, Max found one of those gross-out comedy movies playing on cable. Although he really hated that kind of base humor, he knew kids seemed to like it, so he let Jason watch. It was the first bit of bonding they had done, although very few words were actually spoken. Unfortunately, the movie was only two hours long, and silence filled the air again as soon as the TV was clicked off.

"Your parents should be in Santa Fe by now." Liz checked her watch. "They might be calling soon."

"I wouldn't wait by the phone," Jason replied.

"What is with this attitude?" Liz asked.

"Nothing," he said. "I just don't expect them to call."

"Well, if they do call, I want to ask you a favor," Liz said.

A smile crept to Jason's lips, but it was not warm and inviting. "Go ahead."

Liz sighed. She knew that she could trust the Jason she had grown up with, but whoever it was sitting on the couch with her was totally different from the boy she had known. "It's just . . . they don't know Max is staying here."

"And you want to keep it that way," Jason finished her thought. "Okay."

That was easy.

"What's in it for me?" he added.

Max was caught off guard by the devious mind of the twelve-year-old, but even more surprised by Liz's sudden response.

"How 'bout I let you live until morning." She used a threat that was totally out of character for her, obviously not knowing what else to do.

"I'm going to my room." Jason stood.

When Liz and Max said nothing in response, he left.

They both listened as he stomped up the stairs, remembering back to how they themselves would stomp around their respective homes when they were that age. They waited for the door to slam.

It did.

"That is not the boy I grew up with," Liz said once she knew Jason was well out of earshot.

Body snatchers, Max thought once again, not wanting to make the joke out loud, for fear Liz would think he was making light of the situation. "It's not easy being a boy at this age," he replied. "I know from experience."

"Yeah, but you were dealing with other things too," Liz said.

"That doesn't matter," Max said. "I was still a boy. And I had my dad around to talk to about the nonalien things."

"Somehow Mr. Lyles doesn't seem all that receptive to talking about"—Liz thought for a moment—"well . . . anything." A lightbulb went off in Liz's head. "Maybe he just needs a guy to talk to. Someone closer to his own age."

"I don't know, Liz," Max said skeptically.

"Hey, if anyone can talk to him about changes in life . . . ," she replied.

"With someone he's only just met and hardly said two sentences to?" Max was not excited about the coming conversation. "Maybe he'd rather talk to you. In fact, this could be all about that. He wasn't expecting you to bring a date this weekend."

"He refused to come out of the room before he knew you were here," Liz said. "It's something else." She then hit him with the sad doe eyes that she could do better than anyone Max had ever met.

Moments later, Max found himself heading up the stairs to the second floor and knocking on the door to Jason's bedroom. "Can I come in?"

"No," Jason replied.

Max tried the doorknob, but it was locked again. "Would you like me to open the door like I did last time?"

Max heard footsteps, and then the door lock being turned. *Well, at least that's one small victory.* He waited in the hall, but for reasons he could only assume were territorial in nature, Jason never opened the door. Showing himself into the room, Max found Jason had already made his way back to his bed and had his head buried in a comic book.

The whole point of the weekend was for Max to get an idea of what his own fatherhood was going to be like. As he stood in the doorway looking at a sullen preteen who was trying to ignore him, Max's personal fears were suddenly justified. But he had to ignore those future dilemmas for the time being as he dealt with the problems of a troubled boy whom he hardly knew. And to think he could be in Roswell running from aliens or the FBI right now.

Max decided to play along for a while and take some time to look around Jason's room. He had not really noticed the place earlier when he had gotten Jason to come downstairs, so he gave himself a private tour, hoping to find some clues to the attitude or, at least, some item over which they could bond.

The first thing Max noticed was that, like the rest of the house, this was by far one of the cleanest rooms he had ever seen in his life. There were no clothes littering the floor, and nothing looked out of place. Even the posters on the walls were in frames rather than taped or thumb-tacked up. The more Max found out about Jason, the more intriguing the kid became to him.

Checking out Jason's desk, Max picked up a framed photo of the Lyles family. The three of them were sitting on ATVs in the middle of the desert. At first, it seemed unlikely to Max that the cleanest people he had ever met would go off-roading, but upon closer inspection he noticed that, while Jackie and Jason were covered in dirt, George had somehow managed to remain spotlessly clean. Max assumed that George was just tagging along while the rest of his family and whoever took the picture were out to have fun.

But, most importantly, Max had found their common bond. "You like to ride?" He held the picture out to Jason. "My dad took me out on these same kind of ATVs a few times when I was younger."

Jason turned the page of his comic book.

"He used to call them bicycles with an attitude," Max continued. "Eventually, my dad told me it was getting too expensive to rent them."

"We own ours."

He speaks.

Max considered suggesting that they take a ride out on them this weekend, as a bonding experience. He quickly realized that it was one thing for him to be there in secret, but it was quite another for him to take a twelve-year-old out on a dangerous vehicle without adult supervision. However, he was not going to let the opportunity slip away. "Maybe some weekend when your folks are home, I could come down and go riding with you."

"Whatever."

"No, it'll be fun. I'll ask your mom when she gets back," Max knew he was pushing too hard, but he couldn't help himself.

There was a long pause as he tried to figure out his next move. "What are you reading?" Max tried valiantly to keep the small talk going.

Again, Jason just turned the page.

Wanting to make some kind of connection, Max reached out, placing his hand on Jason's shoulder. The kid immediately pulled away and shot Max an almost murderous look. Then, the hatred in his eyes receded as if he just shook it off. "Please don't touch me," he said with his voice two levels softer than a whisper.

Undaunted, Max continued, but kept a distance so he didn't cross the line again. "Look, Jason. I know we just met," Max pushed ahead in paternal mode, "but if there's anything you want to talk about, you can tell me. . . . Maybe something you'd be more comfortable saying to me than Liz?"

No response.

"Trust me, I know how difficult it can be." Max used his own personal experience, remembering back to the things he had wished someone would have said to him when he'd gone through life changes—though his changes had been a little more extreme than what Jason was going through. "You may think you're alone, but trust me: Every guy has gone through what you're going through."

Jason gave him a look like he honestly had no idea what Max could possibly be talking about.

Not knowing how far he should go with this particular

conversation, Max paced the room as he chose his words carefully. "It's totally natural for these things to happen. You're just moving on to the next stage of your life."

A smirk came across Jason's face as the boy realized exactly what this conversation was about. "What stage?" he asked coyly.

"I think you know what I'm talking about." Max read the boy's expression.

"Is this a sex talk?" Jason spat out.

"No!" Max quickly responded. He wasn't exactly sure how far this discussion was going to go, but he was fairly sure that Jason's parents wouldn't be thrilled if some teen they didn't know suddenly took it upon himself to tell their son all about the birds and the bees. "It's in the same general area, but I don't think that's a discussion you and I should be having. Look, Liz considers you a close friend. And since Liz and I are close friends, she wanted you and me to be friends as well. I'd like that too. And as a friend, I wanted to let you know that if you want to talk about anything . . . if you have any questions about anything . . . I'm here."

"Are you and Liz having sex?" Jason leaned forward, giving his undivided attention for the first time in the conversation.

"I don't think that's really your business, but no." Max didn't intend to answer the question at all, but he did want to make sure that if any of this weekend was relayed back to the parental units, Jason would get that part right.

"Why not?" Jason asked.

"That's *really* none of your business," Max said. "And we're here to discuss you."

"I'm not."

"Well, I am," Max said. "And that's the point I want to make. I know we've just met and you don't know me. But I'll be here for the rest of the weekend if you feel like opening up. Okay?"

Jason took a moment to think about what Max had said. "Okay."

It was a small victory, but Max knew to take whatever he could. "I'll be downstairs if you need me." He made his way to the door, but had one more fatherly piece of advice before he left. "You should get to bed soon. It's getting late."

7

Hours later, when most people in both Artesia *and* Roswell were asleep, there was a loud knocking on Michael Guerin's apartment door. Maria knew that he was home and was not at all happy about how she had left their dinner earlier. Now, she was back to put an end to their fight once and for all.

If Michael would only answer the door.

"Who is it?" he groggily shouted.

"It's me," Maria answered back with a much lighter tone than the last time she was at his door. "Who else would be knocking at two A.M.?"

"Around here? It could be anyone," his muffled voice said.

"Can't argue with that," she conceded, still staring at the closed door. "Are you planning on letting me in?"

"I'm thinking about it," he said, finally opening the door for her.

"Look, I'm here to apologize." She pushed past him and entered the still darkened apartment. Luckily she was familiar enough with the place that she could make her way around without getting hurt. *Far be it for him to turn on a light for me.*

"Apology accepted." He stumbled over to his couch. "Couldn't you have done that over the phone?"

Maria turned on a lamp so she could see, temporarily blinding Michael, which she saw as a minor victory in passive aggression. "No, because I need to explain *why* I'm apologizing."

"Because you were wrong." Michael was always great at cutting right to the chase in any situation. He reached over to turn off the bright light, taking his own little victory from her.

Maria counted to ten and resigned herself to the fact that this discussion was going to be held by the moonlight coming through the window. "I am willing to accept that I was wrong to assume that you would be comfortable performing in front of people."

"Thank you," Michael said. "Can I go back to sleep?"

"But," she continued, "you should have asked for help."

Michael knew that she wasn't going anywhere until she got out what she had come to say. She was persistent like that. Of course, he certainly wasn't going to make it easy for her. "Help doing what?"

"Coming out of your shell," she said, joining him on the couch. "You're always so contained . . . so secretive. You need to bust out more. You don't even belong to any clubs at school."

"I'm not really a joiner," he replied.

"Well, then, it's a good thing you're going out with me." She slapped him on the knee to accentuate her statement.

"That's not the only good thing," he mumbled.

"Funny," she replied, swatting his hand away.

"So, where is this going exactly?"

Even in the darkness, her face could easily be seen beaming with excitement. "I'm going to teach you to sing!"

And for what was definitely one of the rarest occurrences in the life of Michael Guerin, he actually laughed out loud. In fact, he nearly fell off the couch because he was laughing so hard. It was easy to tell that it wasn't genuine laughter, but Maria tried to ignore his inconsiderate response.

She continued, undaunted by his reaction. "No, listen. I'll teach you to sing, and maybe we could even front Alex's old band together."

"And then I could join the school choir," Michael said derisively, "and we could be the leads in the school play. I hear they're talking about doing *West Side Story* next year. I could totally see you as Maria . . . Maria."

Maria immediately realized how ludicrous her own idea sounded when she said it out loud. *Funny how it all worked well in my head.* But she was not ready to give up. "Okay, what about sports? Something to get you out in front of people. Do you know that hardly anyone at school even knows who you are?"

"Yes," Michael replied. "That's how I like it. It takes a hell of a lot of work to be as invisible as I've made myself."

"There's a difference between invisible and nonexistent," she replied.

To Maria, who intended to spend the rest of her life performing in front of others, either idea was an unheard-of concept. As such, she completely ignored him. *If Danny could change for Sandy in* Grease, *then you can certainly change for me.* She knew enough not to say that to him, but she certainly thought it. *And why has this conversation suddenly become about musicals?*

She continued to push. "Come on, there has to be something you're good at."

Leaning back into the couch, he closed his eyes, apparently giving up on the conversation. However, Maria had no intention of ending things without helping him find a way to focus his energy. She obviously knew what was better for him than he did.

Since she expected to be there a while, Maria turned on the light once again, blocking the switch so he could not turn it off. This time, she noticed something that looked as if it had been quickly stashed in the corner with a sheet loosely covering it. *So that's why it took so long for him to open the door.* Getting up from the couch, she walked over to the mysterious object.

"What are you doing?" His eyes were now wide open, and he was off the couch.

She pulled at the cover the same moment he grabbed her arm, but it was too late. The masking fell to the floor, and Maria found what he had been hiding.

It was a painting.

It was beautiful.

"Who did this?" she asked, picking it up. Looking around the room, she pulled a chair over to the couch and leaned the painting on it. While she was up, she also turned on another light to get a better look.

The painting looked to Maria like some kind of abstract . . . or Impressionist piece. If she had ever paid attention in art class, she would have been better versed as to whether either of those terms were even remotely correct ways to refer to the work. But that didn't matter. Whoever had painted it had known just the right way to evoke emotion through the use of color combinations.

The blue background had slashes of red cut through it, and gray streaks ran through the top of the painting, giving the impression of a coming storm. But, down in the lower right-hand corner, there was a small dab of the brightest yellow. It almost looked to Maria like a flower struggling to emerge.

The effect of the painting left Maria feeling both sad and angry at the same time—a feeling that she had felt a lot over the past few months. But there was something more . . . a feeling of hope. In fact, these were the exact same feelings she had experienced when she sang at Alex's funeral. She remembered that because she had felt something similar the other night during the memorial celebration at the Crashdown.

"You painted this," she said with shock in her voice. "But I thought you only cared about art when you were drawing that geodesic dome thing sophomore year."

"I did." Michael joined Maria as she admired the painting. "But when I heard you singing at Alex's funeral, this is how it made me feel. After we had the big fight following the service, I stopped off at the art store on the way home for supplies and did this. I just needed to."

"And you've been keeping this hidden for months," Maria said.

"I wasn't ready for anyone to see it."

He had managed to do it again. No matter how high or low her expectations, Michael always found a way to blow them out of the water. She wondered if there was ever going to be a time when he couldn't surprise her.

And she hoped that time would never come.

"I'm sorry," she whispered.

"You already said that."

"No," she clarified. "I mean, I'm sorry I keep trying to change you. I love you for who you are, Michael Guerin. You may have been genetically engineered to be a soldier, but you have the soul of an artist."

Maria pulled him down on the couch beside her as she stared at the painting. The longer she looked at it, the more she saw and felt. She was amazed that it evoked the same feelings she had hoped her own singing would elicit from others. Hugging Michael to her body, she felt closer to him than she had since the day he chose to remain on Earth for her.

8

As Michael and Maria fell asleep in each other's arms admiring the artwork, Isabel was busy fighting off sleep at the Valenti home as she continued her incredibly long day—and night—with Kyle. Board games, cards, and movies had filled the hours since they had added dinner to their milk shakes at the Crashdown. Isabel had called her parents to let them know that she was safe and would be out late as her intention was to stay with Kyle until he was tired enough to fall asleep on his own.

Isabel was relieved that he had only suffered a few minor flashes throughout the evening, with none of them even coming close to the episode outside the Crashdown when he thought he had seen Alex's car. His fingers continued to drum softly as the two of them watched the credits role on some Jean-Claude Van Damme movie that was on one of the late-night basic cable channels. Even after sitting through the entire movie, she still couldn't think of the title, which was a statement as to how interested she had been in the film. Needless to say, it had not been Isabel's first choice of things to watch, but she'd reminded herself that she was there for Kyle. Besides, she had found other ways to keep herself busy.

Checking her watch, Isabel confirmed that it was two thirty in the morning, and wondered when it would be okay to leave. Kyle was looking rather drowsy, but she wasn't entirely sure that he was finally ready to fall asleep. She had been waiting for him to send her home, but as yet that hadn't happened. If she was going to get up in the morning to go out with Jesse, she was going to need to get at least a couple hours of sleep. Again, she consulted her watch to see that thirty full seconds had passed since she'd last checked the time.

She placed yet another playing card on the rapidly growing structure in front of her. To occupy the slowly moving seconds, she had been constructing a house of cards on the coffee table for the last half hour of the movie. The building was beginning to look quite grand since the design already boasted several levels as well as a few different wings and what appeared to be an Olympic-size swimming pool built to scale. Of course, it would have been more inspiring if she hadn't been using her powers to hold it all together.

"Do you have another deck of cards?" she asked, admiring her architectural accomplishment. "I'm about to run out."

"I think you've done enough," he replied. "If that thing gets any bigger, we're going to need to get a zoning permit."

Two headlights flashed through the living room window as a car, presumably belonging to Kyle's dad, pulled into the driveway.

"Your dad's out pretty late," Isabel said, hoping that he would take the hint and send her home. She felt guilty for the thought the moment it had passed through her mind.

"He's been doing that a lot over the past few days," he replied sleepily, leaning against the arm of the couch. "At first, I thought he had gotten a new job, but he hasn't said anything. He just keeps disappearing a lot, and when he comes home, he's always humming."

"Humming?" she thought about that for a moment. "You know, he was pretty good when he sang with Alex's band the other night. I was quite impressed. And now that I think of it, so was Maria's mom."

"Please, don't remind me," Kyle replied. "I'm just happy I'll never have to witness my father doing a gig with a band ever again. And the less we talk about my dad and Ms. DeLuca, the better."

Jim Valenti entered the house not only humming, but also looking happier than Isabel had seen him in a long time. There was even a bit of a bounce in the way he was walking, like he was moving to the beat of the song in his head. His mind was definitely still back on whatever he had been doing, since he made it halfway into the living room before he realized that he wasn't alone.

"Oh, kids . . . hey." He stopped short as he passed the couch. "Isabel, what are you doing here at this hour?" Checking his watch, there was a sharp change in his mood. "Is something wrong? Where's Max? Did something happen?"

"Dad, relax," Kyle said from the couch. "Everything's fine. We're just hanging out, watching movies, and building a miniature metropolis out of cards."

Valenti was visibly relieved. "Sorry. It's been a pretty quiet week around here, considering. And I get a little nervous waiting for the next thing to happen." Then he saw the structure that was quickly overtaking his coffee table. "I assume that's your handiwork, Isabel."

She nodded but was confused to hear Kyle's father act like nothing was going on, especially considering that his son had obviously been in a lot of pain over the past few days and even weeks. She looked over at Kyle and decided to test the waters. "I know what you mean about being tense. I was finally beginning to relax until this afternoon."

"What happened?" the senior Valenti took the bait.

"Nothing," Kyle stressed in a way that Isabel got the clear message he was sending her to keep quiet. "Nothing but a little paranoia. We thought someone was following us, but it turned out to be a mistake."

"Are you sure?" His father's concern did not subside. "Do you want me to look into it tomorrow?"

For reasons she did not entirely understand, Isabel decided to go along with the entirely fictitious story. "Really, it was nothing more than my imagination," she said. Then she looked at Kyle pointedly, adding, "I feel silly for even mentioning it."

"Yeah, well, you can never be too safe." Valenti yawned. "Sorry. It's been a long night. I should get to bed." He looked at the teens sitting comfortably on the couch and he fell into parental mode. "Will you be getting to bed soon, son?"

"I hope so," he mumbled in response.

"And you, Isabel?" Valenti added in a voice somewhere between stern and lighthearted. "In your own bed, I hope?"

"Dad!" Kyle was shocked and embarrassed by what his father was implying.

Isabel laughed at Kyle's discomfort. Then she blushed because of her own self-consciousness, and the break in her concentration sent the house of cards falling to the ground in pieces.

"Well, it looks like my work here is done." Valenti was pleased with himself for his joke having gotten the reaction he had hoped for. "I was just asking a simple question. You know, my father never would have let me have an attractive girl in the house alone at all hours in the morning."

"Good night, Dad!" Kyle insisted.

"'Night, kids," Valenti replied, and Isabel saw a mischievous smirk on his face.

"Good night," she said, her facial coloring returning to normal as he left the room. Sliding off the couch, she began to pick up the forty-odd cards that were scattered about the floor.

"I'm sorry." Kyle joined her on the ground, apologizing as if he had any control over the words that had come out of his dad's mouth.

Isabel could understand why his father might think something was up. By all appearances, they were the only pair not currently attached to anyone in their incestuous group. She had never really been interested in more than friendship with Kyle, but that's not to say she hadn't on occasion contemplated the possibility. At times, she kind of felt sorry for him, considering his bad luck with women. First Max had taken Liz from him, and later Max kind of took Tess as well. *Then again, maybe it's not bad luck,* she thought. *Maybe it's just my brother.*

At any rate, nothing was going on between them, and she figured nothing ever would. She had managed to find someone outside of the group and was having a good time dating Jesse Ramirez, thinking that it could turn into something more serious and hoping it would.

Once she confirmed that the door to Valenti's room had been firmly shut, Isabel returned to the crisis at hand. "Why haven't you told your father about the dreams?" she whispered, putting her cards back in the box.

"I don't want to worry him." Kyle kept his voice low as well.

"Kyle, he's your dad. It's his job to worry about you."

"I know." He handed Isabel the cards he collected so she could put them away with the others.

Isabel could hear the inaudible "but" hanging in the air. "Go on."

"I'm not the only one he worries about," Kyle reluctantly admitted. "Look at what happened when he walked in the door. The first thing he thought was that something was wrong with you or Max, and he was ready to spring into action. He spends so much time worrying about all of us surviving real threats that I don't need to bother him just because I've had a few sleepless nights."

"What you're going through is more than a touch of insomnia," she reminded him. "But, I understand." And she did. In a way, Valenti had become a surrogate father to the entire group since he was the only adult they had let in on the secret. As such, his concerns for his son had to be split with those for Max, Michael, Liz, Maria, and herself. *Great,* she thought. *Not only did we introduce Kyle to all this craziness, but we stole his father from him as well.*

She tried to push that last thought out of her mind so that her guilt didn't taint any decisions that she suspected she was about to make. The more she thought over Kyle's situation, the more motivated she felt to do something about it.

Crawling back onto the couch, Kyle let out a gaping yawn as his whole body seemed to drag. Isabel suspected that he must have been exhausted since he'd hardly gotten any sleep at all in the past week. She hoped that tonight would break the cycle, and that rest would come soon.

"Do you think you're ready for bed?"

"No," he answered honestly. "I'm not *ready*, but I'm going to have to try. Besides, I'm not going to make you stay up all night."

"I can stay here until you're out," she offered.

"That's okay," he replied, yawning. "I think I'll be fine."

Isabel stood, and Kyle started to rise as well. "No, don't get up." She noticed that he looked like he was about to fall asleep right there, and didn't want him to move. "Just curl up on the couch."

"Okay." He did exactly as she said.

As Isabel made her way to the door, she paused to look back at Kyle. His eyes were drooping, but every time the lids made contact, they kept popping back open. He was so tired, however, that he didn't even notice she was still in the room, which allowed her to stay a few minutes longer to watch. Gradually, his eyes would stay closed for longer increments of time until they finally appeared to shut for good.

Opening the door and letting in a bit of the uncharacteristically cold summer night air, Isabel started to leave when she heard Kyle mumble, "You want me to come along?"

For a moment, she thought he was talking to her, but his eyes were most definitely closed, and his breathing beginning to get shallow. Isabel knew enough from past science classes that it usually took people a while to start dreaming once they fell asleep. She recalled learning that the dreams usually came somewhere around ninety minutes into the sleep cycle. The statistic had stuck in her mind because she had heard it about the same time she had developed a keen interest in learning about anything that was related to sleep, because of her ability to dreamwalk. From that point, she'd tried to learn as much as she could about dreaming and dreamers so that she could be better skilled at the exercise. The fact that Kyle was able to fall into his dreams the moment his eyes closed concerned her a great deal.

As she stared at her sleeping friend, Isabel noticed that Kyle was not only mumbling, but the fingers of his right hand were tapping on the pillow in the same repetitive pattern she had seen before. He was clearly locked into another loop of his nightmare images. She felt horribly for him, but there was nothing she could do about it. Her powers just didn't work that way. It was too dangerous.

Closing the door to the Valenti home, Isabel made her way back to her own house through the chilly night air with those last few thoughts running through her head. They eventually were joined by a renewed sense of guilt over the fact that she and her brother unintentionally had stolen part of Kyle's father from him. Realizing that Kyle's dad was the only parent he really had, it made her feel even worse. Then she thought about all the times that knowing their secret had put Kyle's life in danger, and all the normal things he and his father had given up for them, including the sheriff's job.

And, finally, she thought about Alex.

It didn't take long for Isabel to get home. By the time she had reached the front walk, she knew exactly what she had to do. She tried not to wake her parents as she silently made her way into the house, since she knew they would be getting up in only two hours so they could start their early morning trek to Santa Fe.

Her mother had left the living room light on for her, as she always did, so that Isabel would not have to stumble around in the dark. Turning off the light, she carefully continued through the dimly lit hallway into her bedroom.

With the door gently closed behind her, she turned on her small desk lamp instead of her brighter lamps so there wouldn't be too much light in the room to distract her. Grabbing her yearbook from the shelf, she paused a moment, looking for another book as well. Tucked in between a collection of Shakespeare's sonnets and a largely unused dictionary, she found a book on dream analysis she had bought a while back.

The book had been purchased during the time when she was researching as much as she could about dream images after she'd realized she could visit other people in their nighttime imaginings. For a short time she'd even made a hobby out of analyzing the dreams of some of her friends at school, which often proved to be an entertaining pastime, to say the least. Of course, that was before she'd realized how dangerous it could have been to abuse her powers on recreational activities.

She placed the dream analysis book down on her desk so that she could consult it later, and sat down on her bed with the most recent copy of the *West Roswell High School Yearbook*. Flipping to the photos of the previous year's junior class, she turned to the Vs and found Kyle's photo. On the page, he looked so happy with his frozen smile. The photo had been taken much earlier in the school year—months before Alex's death and Tess's departure.

I'm only going to look around, she thought, justifying her own actions to her conscience. *I just want to get an idea of what's going on in his head, so I can figure out what to do. There's nothing dangerous in that. I do it all the time.*

And yet, her own *sub*conscious was practically screaming out to her that this was not a good idea. *You should wait for your brother to get back,* the intense voice said to her.

Ignoring the inner voices, Isabel placed her right index finger on the photo of Kyle, concentrating on her subject. Closing her eyes, she willed herself into her friend's dreams. Her body relaxed as she could feel her mind leaving on its journey. Slumping down into the bed, the yearbook slipped out of her hands and fell onto the floor.

9

Isabel stood alone in the desert. She didn't recognize the location, but that was not odd, since the miles and miles of dirt surrounding Roswell had a tendency to look the same. Immediately, she wondered if this patch of wasteland was a reflection of a real place from Kyle's past or if it was entirely imagined. Then, she naturally questioned what it could possibly mean. *Could be loneliness,* she thought, *or death. Possibly emptiness or loss or a hundred other things. Maybe I'll just wait to consult the dream analysis book when I wake up.*

Looking over the flat, barren land, she could see for miles, and it was obvious that she was entirely alone. This was strange because, being Kyle's dream, she had expected to see him as soon as she had popped into it. Usually when she dreamwalked, the dreamer was the first person she would see. At the very least, she expected him to arrive shortly after she did. Being alone in the middle of the desert with nowhere to go, all she could do was wait.

"Kyle!" she called out after some time had passed, but received no answer. *What is going on?*

A screech from above directed her attention to the sky. Looking up, Isabel saw what appeared to be a vulture circling ahead—or it could have been a buzzard; she was never really sure what the difference was between the two. One single, solitary bird of prey was waiting just like she was. Another screech came from its beak, letting out a sound that was both strange and familiar to Isabel. It did not make the noise of a bird, but, somehow, it sounded slightly like the high-pitched cry of a woman.

Uncomfortable standing beneath the circling predator, Isabel started walking in the direction she was facing, for lack of any better plan. From her past, limited studies of dreams, she tried again to remember if she had ever read anything that related to what she was seeing, but she was certainly no expert in the field. Instead, she took mental pictures of everything around her so she could look it up in her dream book in the morning. If she didn't find anything there, she was sure there were hundreds more books on the subject. *Maybe Jesse won't mind part of our day together being spent in the library.*

Even though it was only a dream, Isabel could feel the desert heat beginning to rise, but she never felt uncomfortable. No matter how much the heat increased, her skin did not feel like it was burning, and she never even broke a sweat. Out of habit more than anything, she took shelter in the shade of a rock formation. As soon as the sun was blocked and the cool darkness enveloped her, she found herself transported to the Roswell Police Station.

The place was bustling with deputies moving in every direction. It was far busier than she had ever remembered seeing it before, largely with faces of people she didn't recognize, although one or two seemed vaguely familiar. She doubted there was a time in Roswell history that that many police had been on the force at the same time. It was just too crowded for their little town.

Turning a corner, she nearly ran right into Deputy Blackwood. She immediately recognized the Native American who had unintentionally led her and her friends to the Mesaliko reservation two years ago, where they had ultimately found the first real clues to their past. Since he was the first familiar image she had seen, Isabel followed the deputy, hoping he would lead her to Kyle.

"Deputy Blackwood?" she called after him.

"Wait right here," he replied without looking at her.

Isabel wondered if he had actually been speaking to her, since he hardly noticed that she was there. He was busy talking with another deputy behind the front desk and seemed to be ignoring her entirely. While she watched the two police officers carrying out their conversation, Isabel noticed that Deputy Blackwood looked considerably younger than he did the last time she had seen him. She wondered if that was some kind of clue, or if it was just that Kyle remembered the man differently in his dreams. *Remember these are just images,* she thought. *Don't expect it all to be true to life.*

Soon, Isabel grew tired of waiting. "Deputy Blackwood?"

He continued his conversation as if she wasn't there.

"Deputy Blackwood?" she tried again, but still received no answer. She wondered if he even saw her there in the first place. "Great."

Feeling the need to move on, Isabel continued her search

for Kyle in the lobby of the police station. Unable to find her friend, she decided to broaden her search area. Being where she was, she naturally looked for a dream image of Sheriff Valenti as well, but she could not find him, either.

Making her way through the station, she did her best to stay out of the way of the many, many officers tending to their affairs. It did not seem to Isabel that they were in any rush or in an emergency. They all seemed to be going on about their daily business.

In Kyle's dream, the police station was much larger than it was in real life, with winding and twisting halls that simply did not exist. She knew this for a fact, since she was at the Roswell Police Station far more times than any girl her age should have been. Making her way to where she felt was the most logical place to go, Isabel walked a circuitous route to the sheriff's office.

Once she finally reached the office, she found the door closed. As she placed her hand upon the knob, she could hear from within the sounds of a man sobbing. Carefully turning the knob, Isabel pushed the door open and walked right into the Valenti living room.

The crying had stopped.

The room was empty.

Back in the place she had left a short time ago in reality, she found the house looked pretty much the same as when she had been there. There were some notable differences, however. For one, daylight now shone through the windows, making the place much brighter than it had been. Naturally, Kyle was no longer on the couch, where she had left him, although it was made up to look like a bed. Then, she remembered that for the last several months of the school year, the couch had been Kyle's bed. His actual room had been taken over by someone else. A feeling of trepidation came over her as she realized this part of the dream was taking place in the not so distant past.

Again, Isabel checked around for Kyle, but he wasn't in the room. *This is really odd,* she thought. *Where is Kyle?*

Voices.

Coming from Kyle's bedroom.

The voices were familiar and they sounded very angry. Isabel knew exactly what was going on behind the closed door to Kyle's room, but she did not want to see it. At the same time, however, she was drawn to the room. Whether it was because of the dreamwalk or her own curiosity, Isabel could not be sure. But suddenly, the door was open, and she was standing at the threshold about to witness an event that she had her own nightmares about.

It was Alex. Her Alex. The Alex she had tried to ignore for so long, until it was too late. He was in pain, talking about Las Cruces and mindwarps. He could barely stand. His face was twisted in what Isabel could only imagine to be excruciating pain.

Tess was there too. Alex was leaning on her, holding on to her as if he did not have the power to stand on his own. She looked frightened and trapped. There wasn't a trace of the anger Isabel had expected to see, only fear. It had been so much easier to think that Tess had acted out of anger. It made hating her all the more effortless.

Tess turned, looking directly at Isabel. "Kyle, get out!" she yelled, with anger finally creeping into her voice as if Kyle had done something wrong simply by walking into his own bedroom.

But Kyle wasn't standing there, Isabel was.

It was the first time she had seen Tess since she'd found out the truth behind Alex's death. The evil alien had left Earth before Isabel had had a chance to confront her and make her either explain why or suffer for what she had done. And even though Isabel knew that the image standing before her was only a dream, she still wanted to lash out . . . to hurt her . . . to kill her.

Through her own boiling anger, Isabel heard Alex say that he might as well be dead.

"No!" Isabel yelled as if the strength of her voice could stop past events. "Don't say that! Don't wish that!" she screamed, trying to tear him away from Tess, but something held her firmly in her spot. She could not move. She could not stop what was happening.

She could only watch as Tess grabbed Alex's hands and closed her eyes performing the mindwarp . . . the last mindwarp . . . the fatal mindwarp.

"No!" Isabel screamed in unison with Alex.

Still locked in place, Isabel watched Alex crying out in pain, trying to pull away, then falling . . . to the floor . . . to his death.

Isabel broke loose a torrent of sobs. Not even her most horrific dream had prepared her for witnessing the events as they had played out. She had never even imagined the feeling of helplessness Kyle must have experienced watching the scenario unfold and not knowing what was going on, ultimately realizing there was nothing he could have done. An intense feeling of guilt washed over her worse than she had ever felt before.

A moment later, Isabel was dragging a duffel bag. She

was confused by what was going on. *Where is Alex? Did it really happen? Did I really see what I saw?* The bag was heavy, and the weight was unevenly distributed. It didn't feel right to her.

Tess followed as Isabel dragged the bag out of the Valenti house. There was a forced smile on Tess's face, and Isabel knew that she should hate the girl, but couldn't figure out why. She carelessly deposited the bag into the car, stuffing it into the front seat.

Suddenly, realization struck Isabel. It hit with the force of a train. There was no duffel bag. Alex was the *thing* she had loaded into the car. He was the *thing* slumped in the passenger seat . . . broken . . . dead.

"You want me to come along?" she asked Tess without knowing why.

"No," Tess replied in a hollow voice. "Go in the house. I'll take care of everything from here."

Although she wanted to stay, Isabel was drawn back into the house. She did not even stop to look at Alex for a final few seconds as Tess pulled away. She heard the car engine start as, crying, she made her way back through the Valenti home.

I didn't want to see this. I didn't want to live through this.

The pain was unimaginable.

She was back in Kyle's bedroom. Echoes of Tess and Alex resonated through her head. The fight played over in her thoughts. . . . His final words . . . his final scream of pain.

Isabel collapsed onto the floor on the spot where Alex had died, weeping uncontrollably.

Why?

The bedroom door slammed behind her, drawing Isabel's attention away from the empty spot on the floor.

With tears in her eyes and streaming down her face, she looked at the closed door, but there was no one there.

Then she felt his presence in the room before she saw him.

Still on the floor, she wiped the tears from her eyes and looked up at the bed beside her. A small boy was sitting on the edge, with his legs gently swinging back and forth. He was looking down at her, both sad for her and frightened of her at the same time. "It's all my fault," he said in a hollow voice.

Jim Valenti crept silently through his house taking extra care not to wake up his son, who had crashed on the couch. He was used to the hushed puttering around because Kyle used to sleep there regularly while Tess had been staying with them.

Valenti cringed when he thought of his former house-guest. He had taken the seemingly helpless girl into his home and let her live with him and his son as a part of their family and all the while she was using one of their friends and ultimately wound up killing him. Valenti had always prided himself on his detective skills, and still had not managed to get over the fact that he had lived for weeks with a murderer under his own roof.

Pushing the useless regrets out of his head, Valenti took a moment to observe his slumbering son. When Kyle was a child, Valenti used to make a practice out of peering into the boy's room when he would come home late from work, to make sure his son was sleeping soundly. He especially made a habit of it after his wife, Michelle, had left them for parts unknown.

Sitting for a moment on the piano bench, he remembered

back to the time when music had filled the house. He and his former wife would take turns singing their son to sleep on the nights he had come home from work on time. He had forgotten how much he missed the music until recently. The memorial for Alex had been a powerful reminder.

Kyle was tossing on the unmade couch and mumbling slightly. Valenti worried that his son might be having a bad dream, because the way his face was scrunched as if in pain. He remembered back to a time when, as a child, Kyle always looked like a cherub lying under the covers—one of heaven's youngest angels. Valenti chuckled to himself as he thought, *Kyle would love me to describe him that way in front of his friends. I'll have to remember to do that someday.*

Still in silence, Valenti finished up his morning rituals planning for the long day ahead of him, in which he had much to do. Writing a note to his son, he tried to explain what he was up to, but decided on a simple, "Gone out. Be back later," because the full explanation was more than one sheet of paper off the notepad could manage to fit. Valenti left the note on the coffee table, taking one last look at his sleeping son. Then he threw on a light jacket and made his way out the front door, humming as he carefully closed the door behind him.

The slight click of the lock was enough to rouse Kyle from his somewhat troubled sleep. Morning came for him much more slowly than it had in the past few days. Light was streaming through the window warming his face and brightening the darkness behind his eyes. The dreams had not gone away, but somehow they had seemed more manageable, more tolerable. For the first time in weeks, he felt somewhat rested.

Peering through the slits in his eyes, he turned his head to the clock on the wall and saw that he had actually gotten over five hours of uninterrupted sleep. It wasn't a full night, but it was far more than he had slept in a long time.

With a small sense of relief, Kyle fully opened his eyes.

Rolling off the couch and onto the floor, he did his usual quick set of push-ups to get the blood flowing and rouse the body and mind back into full consciousness. He hadn't done this morning ritual in several days, since he was usually too tired to get out of bed, much less attempt any exercising. Today, however, was different. True, he was still somewhat groggy, but at least he felt rested.

Reaching out to the coffee table, he picked up his father's short note and added yet another meaningless clue to the mystery of his dad's disappearing acts. *Oh well, he'll tell me when he's ready,* Kyle thought.

Stretching, he stood and scratched his belly. Taking a deep breath, he felt more awake than he had in days, but still with some residual sleep filling his head. It was taking a while for him to clear his mind and become fully conscious, but at least he wasn't plagued with horrible images. He hoped that the feeling would last the rest of the day, or at least the morning.

Moving to the bathroom, he splashed some cold water on his face to shock himself into consciousness. It seemed to work as his brain slowly came around. He took a long look up at himself in the mirror and was surprised to see he looked happy and far more awake than he actually felt.

This is going to be a good day, he thought as he prepared to start it off—totally unaware of the fact that Isabel was still in his mind.

10

Lying in what must have been the most comfortable bed on this or any other planet, Max was reluctantly waking to the new day. He had heard a buzzing in his ears slowly breaking through his sleep enough for him to think an alarm clock was going off. Realizing that he had set no alarm, Max assumed there was a fly circling his head. He swatted away whatever it was that stole him from his peaceful dreams.

Unfortunately, once the buzzing stopped, he knew that he was too awake to recapture his lost sleep and would have to get out of bed soon. He took a few minutes for the rest of his body to catch up with his now partially aware mind, wondering what new challenges Jason would present today and how he would handle them. *Liz had a great idea,* he thought. *Who could ask for better on-the-job training for fatherhood?*

Just as he was finally ready to pull himself out of bed, Max heard someone knocking.

"Max, are you up?" Liz asked through the door of the

guest room in which Max had spent the night. They had agreed that it would be best if they were sleeping in different rooms in case Jason got up before them. Things were stressful enough already that they didn't need to add anything else into the mix. Not that they would have been doing anything other than sleeping in a shared room, but Jason's young mind probably wouldn't have assumed that their intentions were entirely pure. And the jury was still out on what Liz's young friend would be keeping secret when his parents returned—if anything at all.

"Come in," he said, yawning.

Liz opened the door. "You're still in bed?"

"It *is* Saturday," he reminded her, as if weekdays and weekends really mattered in the summertime. Pulling back the covers, he revealed he was dressed only in a T-shirt and boxers. "How long have you been awake?"

Liz politely turned so he could have some privacy as he slipped into a pair of pants. "Long enough to have eaten my breakfast and gotten a shower."

Max immediately felt guilty for sleeping in. "You should have woken me up."

"I just did," she said with a sly smile. Turning, she went back into the hall. "Don't worry, you can have breakfast with Jason."

"Thanks," he called after her, dreading the idea of another meal spent in silence. *Day two begins.*

Walking only a few steps down the hall, Liz brought herself to Jason's door. Pausing to take a deep breath, she braced herself for whatever response she was about to receive. "Jason, time to get up," she said, knocking. "Jason?"

Max joined her, brushing his hand through his hair to rid himself of bed head. "Let's not start this again," he said under his breath. Turning the knob, he found that the door was unlocked. "Jason, we're coming in."

And they did.

Jason, however, was not in the room.

Max thought the unmade bed looked out of place in the still spotless room. In fact, it was the only thing that indicated a twelve-year-old lived there.

"He must have gone downstairs already," Liz said hopefully.

Max feared otherwise as he remembered the boy's miserable attitude from the night before, but he chose not to say anything for the moment. With a growing sense of dread, he started down the stairs behind Liz, silently willing her to move faster.

They didn't find Jason in the kitchen, either, and there was nothing around to indicate that he had made himself breakfast. The only dishes out were the ones that Liz had already cleaned and left in the drain board to dry. With growing concern, they searched the rest of the first floor from room to room and found nothing.

"Should we try back upstairs?" Liz was trying to remain calm.

"He's not there," Max said, pulling on the shoes he had left in the foyer the night before. "He's not in the house."

"It's a big ranch." Liz grabbed her own shoes. "He's probably out somewhere on the grounds."

"I hope," Max added.

"We're probably just overreacting." Liz tried to put reason behind her positive spin. "He's not a baby. He can get up and go out on his own in the morning without us sending out a search party."

There was a long pause as Max tried to find a way to share her attitude, but failed miserably at it. As such, he chose not to say anything at all.

"He's run away, hasn't he?" Liz finally accepted the suspicion she was trying to ignore.

"We'd better start looking." Max walked to the front door. *Before he gets too far.*

Liz followed in a rush.

The morning air was brisk, but Max could already tell that the day was going to be a little warmer than the rest of the week had been. It was beginning to look like their unseasonably cool summertime was coming to an end—probably not today, but soon. However, Max had far more important things on his mind than the weather. His first official act as a responsible adult and he had lost the child. This did not bode well for his future parenting plans. "Where should we start?" he asked.

"Let's try the rear edge of the property," she suggested. "We can systematically work our way back to the house from there."

Since Liz was only slightly more familiar with the layout than Max, she led the way as they searched the grounds. Relying on her memories of visits from years past, Liz took them across the acres of field as they headed for the back section of the fence that surrounded the property. If Jason had decided to hide on the ranch, he was probably doing so as far away from the house as he could. If that was true, Max hoped that the search would be over in a matter of minutes.

"Did Jason ever mention any places he liked to go? Like a secret fort or a clubhouse?" Max thought back to his own childhood and the castle he had made out of cardboard boxes in the backyard. *Funny how I never realized how appropriate it was for me to have a secret castle.*

Liz scanned her memory, going over past letters and e-mails. "Not that I remember. He hardly ever wrote anything about the ranch. I always thought it was strange since he lived in an apartment in Roswell before moving to this huge place. I know I probably wouldn't have stopped talking about it if I'd had a place with so much room to play when I was his age."

"Seems a little lonely," Max commented as they walked across the field. "So big and empty. Did he ever mention any friends? Maybe he's over at someone's house."

"He never told me about anyone here," Liz said. "But we have been out of touch for over a year, which is like an eternity at his age. He could have a ton of friends . . . or none at all."

"It sounds like his life is about as lonely as Michael's was growing up."

"This is as far as the land goes," Liz said as they came to a fence made of wooden posts with some kind of wire strung between. It didn't appear to be a sturdy fence, but it looked to be strong enough to keep the sheep in.

Max paused for a moment, wondering where the sheep had been. He hadn't seen any since their arrival, although he, Liz, and Jason had been in the house all afternoon yesterday. Off in the distance, he noticed a barn and assumed the sheep were kept safely inside. He remembered something about ranch hands and figured that they should be coming around shortly, if they weren't on the premises already. They could potentially make searching for Jason a much more public event, which had its fair share of positive as well as negative aspects.

Liz looked out onto the adjoining property. A few horses were meandering around aimlessly. "I don't see him anywhere."

"Should we start over there?" Max pointed at the barn.

"It's as good a place as any," Liz said as they started off in that direction.

The barn was set off to the back corner of the property and looked like it had been added much later than the rest of the buildings. Max found that to be odd, since the barn was usually the whole purpose that this type of property existed and was generally kept rather close to the house for obvious reasons. He couldn't help but suspect that the barn had been moved to its present location in recent years considering that having sheep too near the house would probably be in conflict with maintaining its clean exterior.

As they made their way across the field, Max's eyes tracked across the Lyleses' property. There really wasn't much to see other than an open field, the main house, a rather large garage, and a small guest house—which he assumed had once been a house for the ranch hands back in the early days of the property.

Max thought about the guest house and figured that would be their next place to search on the property. He didn't think Jason seemed the type of boy to hide out with the sheep in the barn, but in keeping with their plan to work from the back to the front, it was the first place they would have to rule out. Actually he assumed that Jason wasn't playing a game of hide-and-seek on the property at all. But before they could leave the grounds, they first would have to confirm that Jason wasn't on them.

"Wait a second," Max said as Liz was about to open the big barn doors. "Maybe we should look in the window first and see what's inside. I would hate to open those doors and let a flood of sheep loose."

"Good point." Liz let go of the handle. "We should also check for those ranch hands. It's weird we haven't seen anyone yet."

Max had to climb on top of a barrel to reach the window. Once he managed to get his balance and see inside, he was surprised to find absolutely nothing in the barn. "It's empty," he reported back to Liz.

"No ranch hands?" she asked.

He hopped down off the barrel. "No ranch hands. No sheep. No anything. The place is deserted."

"Who owns a sheep ranch with no sheep?" Liz asked the obvious question.

Max pulled open the doors. "Jason, are you in here?"

Stepping inside, their voices echoed in the emptiness.

"Jason, this isn't funny," Liz added as the words she spoke reverberated off the walls.

"He could be in the loft." Max pointed to a ladder along the back wall that led to the second floor of the barn.

"I'll go check," she said, and started heading to the ladder.

"I can go," Max offered.

"You climbed up on the barrel," she replied. "Now, it's my turn."

"We can both go," he said when they reached the ladder.

"It doesn't take two people to look in an empty loft," she said as she started up the ladder. "Stop being such a gentleman. It's starting to get a little sexist."

"Sorry," he said as he watched her climb the ladder. "Is there anything up there?" he hollered to her.

"Nothing but a bunch of flies!" she yelled back, working her way down.

"Flies." He turned the word over in his mind. "That's it."

"You know where Jason is?" she asked excitedly.

"Not exactly," Max replied, "but I think I know how he got there."

11

He rang the doorbell once again.

Kyle waited outside the Evans home hoping that Isabel would answer. He had experienced his first night of uninterrupted sleep in the longest time and it was all thanks to her generously spending the entire day with him yesterday—as well as a large part of the night. Sure, he still had troublesome dreams, but they did not rouse him from his precious slumber. He knew that he hadn't caught up with all the sleep that he had lost, but it was certainly a start.

Tired of waiting, Kyle started to walk back to his car not knowing what he would do with the rest of his day. He knew that Mr. and Mrs. Evans weren't home, but he hadn't expected Isabel to be out so early since she had stayed up late with him. *Then again, maybe she's not up yet.*

Since he had come over to thank her in person, Kyle figured he should at least confirm that she was, in fact, not in the house. Making his way around the Evans residence, he decided to try what unofficially had become the primary way of entering homes for him and his friends. Peering into

Isabel's window, he confirmed that she, indeed, was still asleep.

Hope no one thinks I'm a Peeping Tom.

Kyle checked around to make sure he wasn't being watched as he was watching Isabel. She looked so peaceful that he decided not to disturb her since he was the reason she was sleeping late that morning. He was about to leave when the inherited detective traits he had received from his father and grandfather kicked in and he noticed several things wrong with what he was seeing.

Isabel was still wearing the same clothes from yesterday, which he did not think to be all that odd considering that she might have been too tired to change when she got home last night. But, as he looked further into the room he also noticed that she must have been too tired to turn off her desk lamp as well. Then there were other bothersome clues that something was wrong, like the fact that she was lying on top of the covers on what Kyle knew had been an exceptionally chilly summer night. Not to mention that her body was sitting up and twisted in what looked to be a very uncomfortable angle for sleeping.

Concerned, Kyle pushed open the window and stepped inside. "Isabel?" he whispered so he could wake her gently. That didn't work. "Isabel?" he tried more loudly, "Isabel!" Moving in, he progressed to shaking her—first gently, then roughly. "Isabel, wake up. Come on, you're scaring me!"

Her head rolled to the side, but her eyes did not open.

Kyle laid Isabel down in a more comfortable pose and frantically searched the room for clues as to why she wouldn't wake up, but found nothing. *What's going on?* He thought of the myriad of reasons why she would not be responding to him. *Alien disease? Body snatchers? Are we under attack? Do these things hibernate?*

Grabbing a hand mirror off her dresser, he tried a trick that he had learned when taking care of his grandfather. Holding the mirror above her lips, he held his breath as he waited for proof of hers. The mirror fogged as Isabel exhaled, confirming that she was alive. With that done, he had no idea what to do next.

Liz.

Seeing Isabel's cordless phone lying on the nightstand, he picked it up and started to dial Liz's home number, but then he remembered that she was out of town and she had taken Max with her. He considered trying her cell phone, but with Artesia an hour away, he was hoping for some more immediate help since he wasn't sure that now was a good time to be alone.

Michael.

But he didn't know that phone number.

Continuing his frenzied search through the room, he tried to find Isabel's phone book, but it wasn't by the phone and he had no idea where she could have put it, if she even had one at all. He gave up on that search, figuring that she probably knew Michael's number by heart and didn't have it written anywhere.

With his father pulling yet another disappearing act and going out before Kyle had even gotten up, there was no reason for him to even try his own home for help. Suddenly, his small group of friends seemed to be considerably smaller.

"Isabel, get up!" he tried again, yelling and shaking her.

He checked her pulse and found it a little slow, but nothing to add to his already growing concern. Her skin felt cool to the touch, indicating that she probably didn't have a fever. "Isabel!"

Nothing.

As he wondered what to do, Kyle thought he heard a noise coming from another part of the house. He was struck with the sudden fear that whatever, or whoever, had done this to Isabel could still be in the house. However, he resisted the temptation to call Sheriff Hanson for help, knowing that if he brought the police to the Evans home he could be asking for more trouble than he was currently facing. Besides, he wasn't even sure if he had heard a noise or if it was just his imagination acting up.

Searching the room again, Kyle grabbed a tennis racket, as it was the only weapon he could find. Peeking out Isabel's door, he began his search of the house, silently cursing himself for not going to get some kind of help first.

Kyle confirmed that the hall was empty before stepping out and crossing into Max's room. Luckily, the door was open, so he could tell there didn't seem to be any surprises in there waiting for him. The room appeared empty, but he searched it anyway since it was the most likely place someone would be hiding if they were looking for something alien related. Exchanging Isabel's tennis racket for Max's baseball bat, he tried the closet but happily found it to be empty. Keeping the bat in his hands, he moved on to the rest of the house.

Making his way through Mr. and Mrs. Evans's bedroom, he continued to find nothing out of the ordinary.

Glad to have the weapon for protection, he took his search through the rest of the house, going from room to room, checking doors and windows as he went. The doors were all locked, but most of the windows were not. However, all of them were closed except for the one Kyle had come through.

Ending his search back in Isabel's room, Kyle let some of the tension release from his body, content to believe he had only been hearing things. He put the bat down in a corner, making sure it was easily accessible in case he needed it later.

Michael.

"I'll be right back," he promised Isabel's prone form, "with help."

Back out the window, Kyle hopped into his car and pointed it in the direction of Michael's apartment. He hated to leave Isabel alone as she was, but he had no choice. If he had been thinking clearly, he would have tried to call Maria. Even if she wasn't home, her mother probably could have given him Michael's number. But Kyle wasn't thinking clearly. He was thinking of the myriad of things that could have put Isabel in her comatose state.

Zooming through the streets of Roswell, he was afraid he might get pulled over by the police. True, he could probably talk any of the deputies out of giving him a ticket, since he had grown up around most of them. But he didn't want to have to waste the time being lectured, since they all still thought of him as a little kid. He silently prayed to Buddha to keep fortune on his side as he headed for Michael's place with his tires screeching at every high-speed turn.

* * *

Deep within the recesses of Kyle's mind, Isabel sat in an exact re-creation of his bedroom. She was no longer alone. A boy sat beside her who appeared to be around six years old—and seemed to be Kyle.

Isabel had known Kyle for years, although they had not been close friends until recent events had thrown them together. She remembered how he had looked the first time she had seen him at school. The small boy who sat beside her on Kyle's bed seemed slightly younger than the Kyle she had met on the playground that fateful day when her friends and she had actually noticed the boys on the junior league football team for the very first time. There was no doubt in her mind that this boy was one and the same.

He sat there silently swinging his feet back and forth. The bed actually squeaked slightly with each swing of the leg, impressing Isabel by the sheer realism of the dream. Other than that, the room was deathly silent. He had not said a word since his cryptic acceptance of the blame.

It's all my fault.

Isabel had lost track of time, but she knew that she must have been in this dreamwalk longer than in any other she had ever experienced. This concerned her on two levels. First, she worried about her own body since her subconscious had never been gone for so long. And second, she worried about what she could be doing to Kyle's already fragile mind. *I was just supposed to look around,* she reminded herself. "Are you sure you don't want to talk?" she asked the boy yet again.

He shook his head.

"Kyle," she said, deciding to take the chance and use his name.

He looked up at her, confirming her suspicions, but remained silent.

"I understand that you might not want to say anything to me right now," she said gently. "But if that's the case, I'm going to have to leave."

Young Kyle Valenti had a momentary flash of fright cross his face, but it was quickly replaced by a firm look of resolve. He seemed determined about something, but it remained a secret known only to him.

His feet continued to kick against the bed in a familiar rhythm.

Tap, tap tap. Tap, tap.

"I'm sorry," she said. "But I'm afraid if I stay any longer I might hurt you."

Hoping to calm the child, Isabel realized that she was only explaining her motivation for leaving to a shadow projected by Kyle's mind, but this was uncharted territory for her. She was even more concerned that she was doing permanent damage with each passing minute she spent in Kyle's subconscious.

Reaching back into herself, Isabel consciously willed her subconscious to return to her body. Closing her eyes, she prepared for the journey, but when she reopened them, instead of finding herself back in her room, she was still in Kyle's bedroom—or, more specifically, in the dream image of Kyle's bedroom.

She tried once again, closing her eyes and welcoming the sensations that she had grown so familiar with in her many past dreamwalks. She reached out for the floating feeling usually associated with the freedom of traveling outside of her own body and sought the safety and reconnection of her return. However, she felt none of those things as her mind remained locked inside Kyle's.

"Why can't I leave?" she asked the boy, trying not to panic both for his sake and her own. *Kyle could wake up soon,* she thought, incorrectly assuming that she was trapped in a nightmare when in reality it had already become a waking dream.

"I don't want you to go." He finally spoke, with childlike innocence typical of his age.

"But I have to," she calmly pleaded. "I've been here too long. It isn't safe. I could be hurting you."

He just stared resolutely.

"Please, Kyle," she begged with a little more agitation creeping up within her. "I promise I'll come back tomorrow night if you want to talk. And every night after that until you feel better."

"No," he said firmly. "I don't want you to go . . . ever."

12

"Where are we going?" Liz called to Max as she tried to keep up with him.

"We're following a hunch." Max stalked his way over the ranch land he and Liz had just traveled, heading back in the direction of the house. Circling around the front, he veered to the right and followed the driveway up the garage. Pulling on each of the two large garage doors, he found that they were both locked. "Do you know where the keys are?" He started to circle the outbuilding, looking for another entranceway.

"I think I saw a set in the kitchen." Liz started to walk back to the house.

"Never mind," he said as he turned the corner and found that a side door had been left wide open, presumably for their benefit.

Liz turned back and followed him into the garage.

Inside they found that it was large enough to fit four cars and was just as spotless as the house had been. There was currently only one actual car in it as well as a space for the big SUV Aunt Jackie and Mr. Lyles had left in. The rest of the garage was taken up by two all-terrain vehicles that looked exactly like the ones in the photo Max had picked up in Jason's room the previous night. Making his way around the car and to the bikes, he immediately noticed that there was enough room between them and the wall to assume that the third bike had been taking up the space until recently.

"I heard a buzzing this morning." Max bent to see a faint tire track on the concrete floor. "I thought it was a fly in my bedroom, but it must have been the sound of Jason's ATV drowned out by my closed window."

"I didn't hear anything," Liz said, wishing she didn't have to contradict him.

"You were probably in the shower," he replied.

She thought that over and suspected he could be right. "Are you sure there were three bikes?"

"Jason has a photo of him and his parents on the bikes." Max searched for more clues to confirm his suspicions. "He said they owned them. Besides, everything in this house is so precisely organized. Don't you think it's a little odd that there's a big empty space between the wall and the bikes, like there's room for a third?"

"Nice deductive work, Sherlock." Liz was genuinely impressed.

A wooden key rack sat on the wall. It was carved in the shape of a dirt bike and had three empty pegs sticking out from it. "He took all the keys."

"Why would they keep the keys right next to the bikes?" Liz wondered out loud. "It would make them pretty easy to steal if someone got into the garage."

"I think that's the point." Max looked at the two remaining ATVs and couldn't help but figure out which one belonged to Mr. Lyles. The bikes were almost identical with their red and black painted designs, but the one he assumed was the property of the head of the house looked like it had never been ridden. It was amazingly clean for something that was built to get dirty. "Although Jason made sure the bikes won't get stolen." He checked the remaining bikes and confirmed that the two missing sets of keys weren't in their ignitions.

"Well, that really shouldn't be a problem." Liz gave him a sly smile.

Wordlessly, Max placed a hand on each of the two remaining bikes, concentrating on the engines that powered them. A soft glow emanated from his palms to the starters. Within moments, the engines were buzzing a louder version of the same sound Max had heard only a short time ago from his comfortable bed. *Why did I ever get up?* he wondered.

Max grabbed a helmet and a set of safety pads that were neatly laid out on a nearby shelf and handed them to Liz. Turning back to the shelf, he grabbed his own equipment and strapped it on, taking a minute to get the bindings done up correctly. "I think I can give you a quick lesson on these things," he said as he laced up the knee pads. "They can be a little dangerous."

But Liz was already geared up and seated atop her bike revving the engine and looking ready to go. She couldn't help but notice the expression of surprise Max had on his face. "I *did* date Kyle Valenti for a summer. What do you think his idea of a fun day out would entail?"

In the same way he knew that Michael had a tendency to shock Maria, he hoped that Liz would never stop surprising him. "Let's go."

Max aimed his right hand at a button on the wall, and the electronic garage door opened in front of them. They pulled the dirt bikes out of the garage and rode the loop of the driveway out to the street. Stopping, they looked in either direction to see if there was any oncoming traffic or possible clues to tell them in which direction Jason had traveled.

"If we go left, that takes us right into town," Max noted skeptically.

"I doubt he'd go there on an ATV," Liz agreed with his unspoken thought.

There was another property directly across the street from them, and Max crossed out that direction as a possibility. To the right they saw there were only a few more ranches to pass before the road opened up into the desert. "He must have gone that way."

"Max, look at this." Liz called his attention to the side of the road. Together they coasted their bikes over.

"Tracks," he said, confirming what she had been pointing out to him.

The set of bike tracks had come off the Lyleses' property and continued down the dirt path along the side of the road. "Now that we know for sure that he left the grounds," Liz said, "maybe we should call the police."

"I don't know." Max's mind was working on another idea as he stared at the tracks. They were fairly deep in the soft ground and seemed like they would be rather easy to follow, at least for a while. "Something's obviously wrong with Jason. If we involve the police, he may never trust us enough to tell us the truth."

Max tried to remember back to a time when he had considered the police to be the first people he could turn to in an emergency. When he was a child, Officer Friendly would often visit his school to give lectures on safety and what to do when strangers approach. He had always felt better knowing that the officer with the calming voice was keeping the town safe. Back then, the police were the good guys and, as such, he had always felt protected under their watchful eyes even when he'd realized that Officer Friendly's real name was Valenti and had actually been the father of one of his classmates.

He still did feel reasonably safe around the police for the most part, but things were more complicated now. Lately, the police were the last people he could go to for help. Max knew he couldn't trust anyone currently in law enforcement—not because they were out to get him, but because it was their responsibility to report anything out of the ordinary. And the situations that Max usually found himself in were certainly out of the ordinary. *At least I know I can trust Officer Friendly again.*

But here, they were dealing with an ordinary case of a missing child. He worried that his lack of trust in the police could easily put Jason's life in jeopardy. However, he had a nagging feeling that if he and Liz followed the trail and found him on their own, it could ultimately help out with whatever his real problem turned out to be.

"I don't know," Liz said, sharing his concerns on both sides. "I'm really worried about Jason."

"Me too," Max replied, still eyeing the set of tracks left

in the sand by the tires of Jason's ATV. "How about we call the police if we don't find him in an hour."

Liz was hesitant to agree.

"I think he wants to be found," Max added.

"Why do you say that?"

"He would have used the road otherwise," Max replied. "He left the tracks in the dirt for us to follow."

"Aren't you just the detective this morning?" She was impressed by the way his mind was working. "But if he wanted us to follow him, why did he take the keys to the bikes?"

Max thought back to the night before, when he had been forced to use his powers to pick the lock to Jason's room. "Because he's a smart kid."

Revving their engines, they started down the side of the road, careful to keep an eye on the tracks as well as on the traffic as they headed out of Artesia. The road wasn't very well traveled, and the wind was light, so they didn't have any problem following the trail that had stayed fairly intact for them. Max graciously allowed Liz to lead the way since she appeared to be more confident on the ATV. *It really has been years since I rode one of these things,* he thought.

Once they passed the last ranch, the tracks veered off into the desert as Max had suspected they would. Again, the lack of wind over the open land worked in their favor as the tracks remained easy to follow.

Liz slowed her bike to a stop and surveyed the land in front of them. It was totally flat for quite a while before little hills popped up off in the distance. "I don't see anything."

"Me neither," Max agreed, pulling up beside her. "But

he did have a bit of a head start on us. We'll ride out for a while, then turn back."

"Okay," she said, rolling the bike forward. "But we'll have to take it slowly. I'm just a novice at this thing."

"You're already doing better than me," he said.

"I noticed." She gave him a wicked grin and picked up the speed on her bike.

As they continued, the trail stayed relatively fresh for them, with only a few spots where it was obscured by underbrush or the light wind had simply blown sections of it away. Jason had been riding in pretty much a straight line, which was further proof to Max that the boy wanted to be found. Both Max and Liz continued at a safe pace to make sure they didn't lose the trail or hurt themselves.

After about fifteen minutes of riding, they had reached the area dotted with small hills that were somewhat similar to sand dunes. The change in their path forced them to be even more careful of where they were riding. Max had moved into the lead position, but the amount of care he was taking as he rode didn't prepare him when he reached the crest of a hill and lost the trail as well as the ground beneath him.

The bike jumped into the air as Max looked down to see a gaping hole directly under his rear tires. He threw his hand back and a familiar green force field spread beneath him as he and the bike came crashing down upon it. Tumbling from the bike, he managed to keep his concentration focused on the force field so it did not drop him down the dark hole.

"Max!" Liz yelled seconds later as she, too, was airborne.

Sliding his body to the side, he watched as Liz crashed down onto the shield where he had just been lying. He was impressed by how she managed the seemingly impossible task of staying on her bike, although she looked more than a little rattled by the jarring experience.

"Are you okay?" His voice was trembling with concern for her.

She nodded her head deliberately.

The force field continued to hold, protecting them from the dark cavern that lay directly beneath them.

"Hurry up," he said, pushing Liz and her bike off the shield. "I don't know how long this will hold." He knew firsthand that his force fields were good for repelling bullets and evil alien beams, but he wasn't sure how long it could support the combined weight of Liz, him, and the pair of ATVs.

As soon as Liz and her bike were on solid ground, he used his free hand to pull his bike and himself off the green force field. Breathing a sigh of relief, he allowed the power of the force field to return to his body. Now, only a big hole with some ratty looking wooden beams lying across it sat in front of them.

"What is that doing here?" Max asked, still catching his breath.

"Must be an old mine," Liz replied, looking at the big hole. "They're all over the desert."

"You'd think there'd be a sign or something," he said, looking for some type of warning but finding nothing.

"You'd think," she agreed.

They were standing on what looked very much like a

crater, with dirt rising around it on all sides. However, instead of finding a sloping depression in the ground, a dark crevice opened up beneath them. The chasm was about twenty feet in diameter and had several rows of rather loose-looking beams stretched across the top with several gaps of varying widths between them.

At roughly the same point where Max and Liz had come crashing down on their ATVs, several of the beams were broken through, revealing nothing but darkness below.

To Max, calling it a mine seemed wrong somehow. A mine evoked pictures of a large opening cut into the side of a mountain with wooden beams forming an arch that marked the entryway with maybe a set of tracks leading inside. He had seen that type of mine often in old movies and cartoons. But what he was looking at now was not the type of place that Wile E. Coyote would have dreamed up or Indiana Jones would have explored. This was, quite literally, a hole in the ground.

Looking back down the hill, Max confirmed that the tracks they were following did indeed lead in this direction. *Jason definitely came this way,* he thought, but was too afraid to suggest what he was thinking to Liz. He didn't want to know if his suspicions were true and, more importantly, he didn't want her to know.

"Hello! Is someone up there!" a familiar young voice yelled from deep inside the mine shaft. "Help!"

Max was relieved at hearing the voice that confirmed Jason was still alive.

"Jason, is that you?" Liz screamed back, on the edge of panic.

"Liz? Help!" Jason was past the edge.

"Hold on!" Max called back while he searched the area for anything he could use to make a ladder or some kind of rope. "We'll get you out. How far is it to the bottom?"

"I don't know!" Jason yelled back. "I'm not on the bottom."

"What do you mean?" Liz asked, straining to see into the darkness beneath her. "Where are you?"

"I'm on some kind of beam," he replied. "But my bike fell to the bottom. It . . . it sounds really far."

Max could hear Jason's voice trembling as it echoed up the walls of the shaft.

"We'll get you out of there," Max promised.

"Hurry," Jason replied. "I think the beam is going to fall!"

13

Opening her tired eyes, the first thing Maria saw was the beautiful painting still sitting directly in front of her.

The second thing she saw was the light coming in through the window.

And, naturally, the third thing she saw was the clock.

"Michael! It's morning!" she screamed, waking her sleeping boyfriend. "How could you let me fall asleep? My mom is going to kill me. Then she's going to kill you. And then she's going to kill the both of us again, just for the heck of it."

"What?" He slowly came around to her shrill yells, not having heard a word of what she had just said.

"Morning." She slowly summed it up for him in a clear and concise manner. "My mom. Me. You. Dead."

"Well, we can't do anything about it now," he replied. He wanted to turn over and go back to sleep, but he couldn't because he was sitting up on the couch. His neck ached because of the awkward angle he had slept at.

Maria calmed herself, knowing that he was right. Feeling

morning breath overtaking her mouth, Maria reached in her purse for some mints. "I swear, one of these days I'm going to give that woman a heart attack."

"Since you're here," Michael tested the waters, "how about making some breakfast?"

She glared at him in response, crunching on the mint.

"Kidding," he replied defensively, and got off the couch, moving into the kitchen. "You cooked last night. It's my turn this morning. What would you like? And keep in mind I only have eggs."

"Michael Guerin?" She was shocked by the question. "Offering to make me breakfast? The world must be coming to an end. Have you been taken over by an alien . . . oh wait . . . never mind."

"It's a limited time offer only." He had no patience for her sarcasm first thing in the morning. He had no patience for *anything* first thing in the morning—or at most points in the day.

"I would love breakfast." She leaned in to kiss him, but stopped short before making contact. "Ewww. Have a mint." She handed him an extra breath freshener from the pack in her hand. The romantic mood ended, she released him from her embrace, and sat back on the couch admiring the wonderful painting as he went to the refrigerator to find out what was in there that he could use to make breakfast.

"You know, we could probably have a showing of your art in one of those galleries along Main Street," she suggested with mounting excitement. "Or we could do it at the Crashdown. It would be a great gimmick—the cook-slash-artist. The local papers love that human interest stuff, and Mr. Parker would probably love the free advertising for the place. We could put all your work on display."

"All what work?" He was afraid where this was going. "It's one painting."

"Sure, *now*," she replied, moving into the kitchen with him. "But I think you've got this artist in you struggling to emerge. All you need is my inspiration. Think of me as your muse."

"Not interested."

"You haven't even thought about it," she whined. "Artists can make a lot of money."

"Once they're dead," he said, reminding her of the odds of successful living artists. "Like I said, I'm not interested. What happened to the promise you made last night to stop trying to change me?"

"I was emotionally touched by the painting at the time," she explained. "The moment passed. So, do you think you're more into oils or acrylics?"

"I'm more into being left—"

Michael didn't have the chance to continue his thought, because someone frantically started banging on his door.

Maria started to open her mouth to respond, but Michael quickly covered it with his hand. The look of anxiety on his face begged her to remain silent, and she gladly agreed. His biggest fear was that one day the wild pounding on his door would be the FBI . . . or worse. It was actually a fear that he had encountered in the past and was not in a hurry to repeat.

"Michael, it's Kyle. Let me in. Quick!"

Michael and Maria let out heavy sighs of relief as he

removed his hand from her face. "Don't ever bang on my door like that," Michael said as he opened the door to find an out-of-breath Kyle.

"Isabel's in trouble," was all he could say.

After finally catching his breath following the sprint from his car, Kyle quickly detailed the situation of his finding Isabel in her comatose state. Breakfast forgotten, the three of them were out the door as Kyle returned to his convertible while Maria and Michael went to follow him back to the Evans home in her mother's Jetta.

Unaware of the fact that Isabel was trapped in his mind, Kyle led his friends back to her unconscious body, reentering the house by way of her window. He stood over her bed while Michael studied her prone form, not really knowing what to do. Regretfully, this was not the first time they found themselves in a situation where they didn't have a clue how to proceed.

"You found her like this?" Michael asked anxiously.

"Well, she was kind of slumped over," Kyle explained, "but I just straightened her out a little."

Sitting beside her, Michael placed his hand on Isabel's forehead. "She doesn't feel warm. Her face isn't flushed." He took her by the wrist and felt for a pulse. It seemed fine to him—neither noticeably fast nor slow. Her chest was rising and falling steadily. "Was she sick yesterday?" he asked.

"No. Not at all," Kyle quickly replied. "She was fine."

"Did you see anyone strange hanging around?" Michael pressed on. "Following you?"

"No one," Kyle answered. "No one at all."

"And she spent the entire day with you?"

"Well, she did disappear for a few minutes to run an errand, but she wasn't gone long at all. Nothing seemed wrong when she got back, either."

Having come in through the window, neither of them noticed the yearbook on the floor, hiding slightly under the other side of the bed.

"I can't get Liz or Max on their cell phones." Maria came back into the room from the hall carrying her own cell phone, also oblivious to the clue hiding out of her eyesight. "They must be out of the service area, but I left messages. I also called the number Liz gave me for her friends' place. They have to check at least one of those phones eventually."

"Did she give you the address?" Kyle asked, relieved now that he had someone to help him with the crazy situation. "I could go get them. Artesia's only about an hour away."

"I don't know the address." Maria readied her fingers on the cell phone to hit a preprogrammed number. "But I could ask her mom."

"No parents," Michael stopped her. "The more people who know about this, the worse things can get."

Maria sat on the bed opposite Michael and performed her own check for life signs just to confirm everything for herself. "We should think about maybe taking her to the hospital."

"And then what?" Michael's usual hostility intensified the more frustrated he became by the lack of action. "Let them run tests? Maybe draw some blood? Good idea, Maria."

Even though she was used to his antagonistic attitude, Maria was still hurt by Michael's words, but she tried not to show it, knowing he was already under a tremendous amount of stress. "Well, the next person we let in on our little secret had better be a doctor . . . preferably a world-renowned surgeon who specializes in bizarre cases. I'm tired of relying on guessing games and Native American rituals."

"Maria, you're a genius," Michael said, giving a rare compliment as he got up off the bed and moved to the window. "I'll be right back. Kyle, can I borrow your car?"

"Why not take the Jetta?" Maria offered up her mom's car instead since it was parked right next to Kyle's.

"Take the old beat-up Jetta over a Mustang convertible?" Michael was already straddling the windowsill. "Are you out of your mind?"

"Hey, remember who's to blame for the Jetta being so beat up," she replied.

"Kyle?" Michael was still waiting for an answer.

"Sure," Kyle said, fishing in his pocket. "Here are the keys."

"Don't need 'em." Michael was gone before Kyle could even reply.

"I guess that's what it means to be second in command," Maria said regarding her boyfriend's quick exit. "And to think I always dreamed of falling in love with a mysterious man of action."

Kyle took Michael's place sitting on the bed, and gently stroked Isabel's hair. "I don't get it. Nothing alien happened at all yesterday. What could have occurred between my place and here?"

"In Roswell? It could have been anything," Maria replied. "I mean, really, take your pick. We got aliens, alien hunters, Feds, Skins, and even a not-so-crazy self-made millionaire who owns the UFO Center."

The silence that fell over the room was broken by the doorbell.

Kyle and Maria froze.

"Don't look at me," Maria said. "I'm not going to get it."

"Do you think Michael forgot something?" Kyle innocently asked, wondering whether he should answer.

"He's not really a doorbell kind of guy," Maria said. "Or a front door kind of guy, for that matter."

"Wait here," Kyle replied. "I'll see who it is."

Making his way through the house, Kyle wondered who could be at the door, since all of the members of their inner circle were currently accounted for except for his dad. In vain, he hoped it could be someone soliciting charity donations, selling cleaning supplies door to door, or anyone else who would not ask for an explanation for what he was doing answering the Evanses' door. He tried to come up with excuses as he walked through the house, but realized he didn't have a clue what to say.

The bell rang once again as Kyle unlocked the door and turned the knob. Swinging the door open, Kyle initially thought he had lucked out, since it wasn't someone he immediately recognized. *Please be selling something,* he thought once again. Then, a slow realization crossed his mind as he thought he recognized the face as being slightly familiar.

The man standing at the threshold to the Evans home was Hispanic and appeared to be only a few years older than Kyle. He was dressed casually in a polo shirt and khakis, but the image that popped briefly into Kyle's conscious mind had the man dressed in a suit. That was the image that did it for Kyle. He knew it was one of Mr. Evans's employees.

What's his name? Kyle thought to himself . . . *Jesse something?*

14

"I'm going to call for help," Liz said, pulling her cell phone out of her pocket.

"Wait a minute." Max's mind was racing as dozens of scenarios played out in his head, although none of them ended well. "Maybe there's something we can do first."

"Max, you heard him." She ignored the phone for a moment. "The beam is loose. He could fall any minute. We have to get someone out here."

He knew she was right, but he also knew that if she made the call, their situation would immediately spiral out of control. "Liz, whoever we call is going to alert the media. Think about it . . . a kid trapped in a mine shaft. They eat this kind of thing up. We're talking national news. Our faces will be plastered everywhere, and I'm not just worrying about Jason's parents finding out I stayed the weekend."

Liz stared at him blankly.

Then Max stopped for a moment to truly understand what he had just said. *I'm putting my secret ahead of Jason,* he realized. *I'm risking his life to protect my own.* Without thinking about it further, Max reversed his decision. "Make the call."

"Okay," Liz said, "but then you've got to get out of here. I'll handle everything on my own."

"No," Max replied. "I'm not going to leave him."

Knowing she was wasting time, Liz picked up the phone and switched it on, dialing 911 without noticing that the numbers weren't beeping as she pressed them. When she held the phone to her ear, the realization struck her with horror. "My cell's not working."

"Here, try mine." Max pulled his out and handed it to her.

Pressing the "on" button, she quickly discovered that it was also out of the service area.

"What are we going to do?" she asked, handing his phone to him and placing her own back in her pocket without realizing that both of them had irretrievable messages waiting. Into the hole, she yelled, "Hold on, Jason! I'm going to get help. Max will stay here with you."

Jason suddenly screamed.

"What's wrong?" Liz yelled.

"The beam is slipping!" he hollered back.

"Jason!" Liz and Max yelled in unison.

"I'm okay," he hollered back, a little more calmly. "It stopped."

"How far down are you?" Max was readying a plan of his own, removing his pads to give himself more maneuverability, but keeping the helmet on.

"I don't know!" Jason replied. "Not too far."

"I'm going down to get him," Max calmly said to Liz as

he circled the hole. He found a point along the edge where there was enough space between two of the beams for him to easily fit his body.

"How?" Liz was concerned about the risk involved, but even more concerned for Jason's safety. "We don't have any rope."

"I can create handholds in the wall." Max peered into the hole so she couldn't see the fear in his eyes. "It will be just like climbing a ladder."

"It's too dangerous."

"It's our only choice," he insisted.

Liz felt helpless. "Be careful." She gave him a kiss for luck.

"Aren't I always?" He shot her a comforting smile.

Turning, he started down the mine shaft.

Max carefully kicked his feet into the wall of the mine shaft. Holding for a moment, he allowed the dirt to form around his shoes as he used his alien powers to manipulate the molecular structure of the soil and harden it into a strong foothold. Then, he lowered his hands and did the same, curling his fingers into the wall of the shaft so the handhold would give him something to grasp on to.

Slowly and methodically, he repeated the procedure as he made his way down the side of the mine shaft. As he went, he made sure to keep the handholds and footholds close together since Jason would need to use them on the way up and he was slightly shorter than Max.

The sun was rising higher in the sky as more and more light filled into the mine shaft. Max couldn't quite make out Jason's form below him, but his eyes were beginning to adjust to the darkness. As he continued the descent he thought he could see the outline of a body in the shadows below. "Jason, I need you to talk to me so I know when I'm getting close."

"You're almost here," Jason replied, looking up at him. "I can make you out against the light coming from the opening. You look kind of like Spider-Man clinging onto the wall there."

Max beamed at the reference, considering that high praise from Jason. There were many times in the past when he'd secretly compared his alien powers with those of comic book superheroes. In fact, when he was younger, before he'd realized the truth, he'd thought that maybe he was a superhero himself when his abilities started to present themselves. He had even drawn up designs for his own costume. He supposed that, technically speaking, the concept of an alien sent to Earth where he exhibits unusual powers did kind of fall into the superhero archetype.

"I'll have you out of here in a few minutes," Max said reassuringly. "You'll be home in no time."

"No," came Jason's reply.

Max paused where he was, clinging to the wall. "What was that?"

"I don't want to go home," Jason replied.

Recalling the clearly visible path that had led them to Jason, Max had to disagree. "I don't think that's true."

"I wrecked my bike," Jason replied, his hollow voice sounding much closer. "George is going to kill me."

Max continued his climb and could now see Jason sitting on a collection of weak-looking cross beams. He was pleased to see that his young charge had had the foresight to be wearing his helmet and pads when he had sneaked off on his bike. "I'm sure he'll just be happy that you're okay," he said.

"You don't know him."

Max examined the layout, trying to figure out the best way to get him off the beam. Jason was about four feet away from him, but in Max's current position there was only air between him and the boy. "Let's talk about this once we're out of this hole."

Jason didn't reply.

"How did you manage to get caught on the beam?"

"There used to be a bunch more, going all the way across to where you are now," Jason calmly explained. "My bike landed on them. I could tell they weren't strong enough to hold it, so I jumped off. The bike went crashing down only a few minutes later. It sounds *really* far to the bottom."

Eyeing the remaining beams that sagged under Jason's considerably lightweight body, Max could easily tell that they would not support the boy much longer. And it was also clear they could not handle his added weight, either. He would need Jason to slide over to the wall. The only problem was that Max had come down nowhere near the point where the beams met the wall.

"I'm going to have to come around to that side." Max freed his right hand from the wall to point to the direction he was about to move. "Stay exactly where you are until I get there."

"Okay," Jason replied.

Instead of placing his hand back in the handhold he had taken it from, Max stretched as far as he could to the right to get another grip into the wall. He followed that with his right foot. Then, he placed his left hand and left foot in the holes he had just vacated. The beam was now only about five or six feet away. Removing his right hand from the wall again, Max repeated his move, but instead of creating a small handhold, the dirt wall started to fall away in large chunks.

Throwing his weight back to the left, Max regained his balance, but the wall continued to crumble. Focusing his power through his hands, he tried to will the wall back into place, but he could not stop the natural displacement of dirt.

Both Max and Jason followed the dirt avalanche with their eyes wide as it slid closer to the point where the wooden beams met the wall.

"Jason, hold on!" Max yelled as he went back to the position he had been in before he started moving to the side.

Jason lay on his stomach and tightly hugged the beam he was on.

The dirt wall deteriorated at an alarming rate.

The end of the beam began to slide down the wall.

Max aimed his hand at a point several inches beneath the beam, readying himself to use his force field. He hoped he wouldn't have to deploy it in front of Jason, but he knew that exposing his powers to the boy was far more preferable to watching him fall to his death.

One of the wooden beams behind Jason slipped out of the wall and started a long fall to the bottom. Max could hear it hit ground, and agreed that Jason was right when he'd said it had been a considerable drop.

Fortunately the wall stopped crumbling and the beam

Jason was on came to rest after only sliding a few inches. Max stayed where he was, afraid to move either left or right. He knew that the part of the wall he was on was stable. He had seen to it as he climbed down by using his powers to manipulate the molecular structure of the wall, but he was afraid to touch the loose dirt to the side of him for fear of it all falling away once again.

"Okay, we're going to have to go to Plan B." Max reached out his arm to check the distance between himself and Jason.

"I'm not going to like this, am I?" the boy asked.

"You'll be fine." Max paused to convince himself that Plan B was, in fact, a viable option. He realized that there really was no other choice. "I'm going to need you to jump to me."

"Are you crazy?"

Max tried to keep his voice calm, although his entire body was trembling as he considered what they were about to do. "It's only a couple feet. I've got a good hold on the wall. It will be okay." He wasn't entirely telling the truth, because his body was beginning to tire from the strenuous activity, but he knew that he would have to keep going for Jason's sake as well as his own.

Jason looked down beneath them. Although Max knew the boy couldn't see the bottom, they both were aware of the minimum distance the drop had to be based on the length of time it had taken for the beam to crash to the ground. When Jason looked back up, Max could see even more fear in his eyes.

"I can't do it," Jason said, still hugging the beam and shaking his head vigorously.

As if to help Max convince him, the beam slid another inch.

"You've got to," Max said in a forced calm voice. "Trust me."

Jason looked up at the teen he had hardly even met.

Max could only meet his gaze, trying to be both forceful and calming at the same time. He hoped that his face showed the look of someone Jason could trust.

"Okay," Jason resolved. "I'll do it."

Max let out a sigh of relief. "Good. Now, I need you to stand up slowly."

Jason did as he was told, balancing himself on the unstable beam.

"All right," Max said, continuing to use the ultra calming voice. "When you jump to me, you're going to have to use the wood to push yourself off. That means you're going to be adding extra pressure."

"Which means the beam is going to collapse." Jason completed the thought with his voice shaking.

"So you're going to have to move quickly," Max concurred. "No hesitation. No turning back."

"I can do it," Jason said firmly as he obviously tried to convince himself to believe what he was saying. Although Max could still hear the hesitation, he knew that Jason was ready.

Max removed his right hand and foot from the wall and leaned back to the left so he could form a pocket for Jason to jump into. "I want you to throw yourself into my body. I'll grab you as soon as you hit."

"Can't I just reach for your hand?" Jason asked.

But Max had considered that option and was afraid that

even if Jason did manage to clasp onto the small target, his skinny hand would slip right out of Max's grip. "This will work fine."

Jason looked unsure, but determined.

"On three," Max said, preparing his body to take the impact when Jason hit. "One . . . two . . . three!"

Jason launched himself off the beam.

The beam tore away from the wall.

The boy's body slammed into both Max and the wall at the same time.

Max threw his right arm around Jason and turned his own body into the wall.

The beam crashed down many, many feet below.

Jason was cradled in Max's body and pressed up against the wall. They were both breathing heavily and holding tightly onto the wall. As the realization struck them that they had been successful in what they had just done, both boys started laughing uncontrollably.

"Max! Jason! Is everything all right!" Liz screamed from above. Obviously she had heard the crash.

"We're fine!" Max hollered back up to her as the laughing subsided.

He looked to Jason to confirm that he was "fine," and found him to be shaking and breathing heavily, but surprisingly unscathed.

"Time to make like Spider-Man," Max said with a look of relief. "The hard part's over. Let's get out of here."

Still cradling himself in Max's body, Jason turned around to face the wall. Max instructed him on how to use the handholds and footholds that he had left behind on the way down, hoping that Jason just assumed they were a part of the original shaft design. Either way, he did not question their escape route as they slowly made their ascent to freedom, thirty feet above.

"I don't know whether to hug you or hurt you," Liz said with relief as she saw Jason's head pop out of the hole.

"I think he's been punished enough," Max said, pulling himself up onto solid ground, still shaking.

As soon as Jason had found his footing and moved away from the hole, Liz wrapped him up in the biggest hug she could muster. Jason flinched as she squeezed, causing her to let go immediately.

"Are you okay?" Her concern came back as she saw him nursing his shoulder.

"Yes," he said quickly.

"Let me see." She leaned to him, attempting to pull the neck of his shirt aside, but he struggled against her. "Jason, hold still." She held tightly to him and finally managed to tug the shirt away from his shoulder, revealing a huge bruise.

Suddenly, all the pieces fell into place for Max.

"We should get you to a doctor," Liz said.

"It's okay," Jason replied. "Really."

"But you could have a serious injury from the fall," Liz said. "That bruise doesn't look good."

Jason said nothing in response.

"That mark isn't from the fall, is it?" Max asked, almost rhetorically, since he suspected that he knew the answer.

Jason sat on the ground, but still remained silent.

"You had it last night, didn't you?" Max gently prodded.

Liz looked at Max questioningly as they both sat on either side of their young friend. She had no idea what he was talking about.

"You pulled away when I touched your shoulder last night too," Max recalled. "I thought it was because you just didn't like to be touched, but I had hurt you when I grabbed the bruise."

"Is that true?" Liz asked, obviously concerned. "What happened?"

"Was it George?" Max carefully continued the questioning, choosing the most likely suspect.

Jason nodded, refusing to look at either of them.

Liz looked to Max, afraid that the situation was out of their league, but too concerned to let her fears get in the way of helping her friend. "How long has this been going on?"

Again, no answer came.

"Jason, say something," Liz pleaded. She was obviously upset by the surprise revelation. "Please. I want to help you."

Max placed his hand on her shoulder as if to say, *That's enough.*

Liz looked into her boyfriend's eyes. He could tell that she was hurt and confused. Max knew that she was probably blaming herself for not realizing what was happening sooner. He gave her shoulder a supportive squeeze.

"It's okay if you don't want to talk about it right now," Max said. "And it doesn't matter how long it's been going on. It won't happen anymore. We'll make sure of that."

Liz added to his sense of conviction. "I promise you."

"Now, do you have a family doctor we can take you to?" Max asked. "I want to make sure you didn't hurt yourself in the fall." Then, he silently added to himself, *and to make sure Mr. Lyles hasn't done any permanent damage.*

Jason nodded his head.

Max got up and gave a hand to both Liz and Jason to help them off the ground. Hopping onto the bike, he made sure there was room for Jason to fit behind him. Once the boy was safely on, Max turned back to him. "Keys?"

Fishing in his pocket, Jason pulled out two sets of keys. "How did you . . ."

Max flashed him a cryptic smile and took the keys out of Jason's hand, tossing one set to Liz and starting his own bike with the other.

Grabbing the keys, Liz got on her bike and started it up. As the trio started back through the desert, neither Max nor Liz gave any thought to the cell phones in their pockets that were still out of the service area and storing some very important voice mail messages.

15

"Hello," Kyle said, still holding on to the door, making sure the visitor could not see inside—not that there was anything to see, but just in case something odd happened. This was a valid concern, considering the group's history. They never knew when something strange could be going on behind them.

Jesse was naturally surprised to see the stranger instead of Isabel opening the door, but he recovered quickly. "Hi, I'm looking for . . . for Phillip Evans. I work with him."

"Yeah," Kyle stalled while trying to come up with a good cover story. "I know. You're Jesse, right?"

"Yes," Jesse replied.

"I'm Kyle." He held out a hand to the interloper while keeping the other hand firmly on the door. "I'm one of Isabel and Max's friends. How are you?"

"Good," Jesse replied, trying discretely to peek through the partially open door. "Is Phillip home?"

"Actually, no," Kyle responded abruptly, faced with at least one question he could easily answer. "He and Mrs. Evans are down in Santa Fe for the day."

Jesse feigned surprise. "That's right. I forgot. They went to that arts festival."

"Right." Kyle hoped this piece of information would send the visitor on his way. "I can take a message for when they get back. Is there something you needed?"

"I just wanted to talk about a case we're working on." Jesse created his own cover story as he grew more concerned that Isabel had not come to the door yet to rescue him from this situation.

"You couldn't have called?" Kyle asked, suddenly suspicious. Between being the son of a former sheriff and all the alien conspiracy stuff going on in recent history, Kyle's senses were honed to picking up on any kind of questionable behavior.

"I was in the neighborhood," Jesse replied, growing suspicious himself that no one with the name Evans had come to see who was at the door yet. Odder still since Isabel *was* expecting him. "Since I'm here, I was wondering if I could just pop in and say hi to Isabel . . . and Max."

"Max isn't here," Kyle replied, grasping for some excuse. "And Isabel . . . is a little under the weather."

Jesse was instantly concerned, remembering that she had cancelled on him the previous evening to look after a friend she had said was really sick. Unaware of the fact that he was speaking to the sick friend, he tried not to appear too worried, especially since they were only supposed to be passing acquaintances. "I hope it's nothing serious."

"Not really," Kyle flat out lied.

"Would it be okay if I stopped in to say hi?" Jesse moved toward the door.

Kyle, however, stayed firmly planted in place. "Actually, she's resting right now. She said she didn't want to be disturbed."

"By anyone?" Jesse let the charade slip for a brief moment, confused that she hadn't called him to stop him from coming over or alerted this kid to the fact that he might be stopping by.

"Yeah," Kyle said, growing even more suspicious. "If you don't mind, I should get back inside in case she wakes up and needs something."

"Are you sure it's not serious?" Jesse asked, his anxiety beginning to take over and push their whole hidden relationship out in the open.

"Positive," Kyle said, trying not to stretch the lie too far. "We called the family doctor and he just said to let her get some rest. Nothing to worry about."

"Okay." Jesse felt some minor relief. "When she wakes up, please let her know I was here . . . to say hi."

"Will do." Kyle closed the door before anything else could be said in their odd little interaction. He would have to make sure to fill Isabel in on his lie when she woke up, so that no one would question her about it later. *That's the problem with lies—even the simple ones require tremendous attention to detail. Of course, that's all assuming that Isabel would wake up. Don't even think like that.*

"Who was at the door?" Maria asked as Kyle came back into the bedroom. She was sitting beside Isabel, holding her hand and rubbing it in small circles with her thumb.

"Someone from Mr. Evans's firm," Kyle replied. "Nothing important. Any change?"

"No," Maria replied hopelessly. "And I still haven't been

able to get in touch with Max or Liz. Meanwhile, Michael's still off God knows where. Have you tried your dad?"

"He's pulled another one of his disappearing acts," Kyle said, wondering once again where his father was spending his time lately. "I've hardly seen him at all this week."

"What is it with the parents in this town?" Maria asked, frustrated. "They're never around when you need them."

Kyle nodded in agreement.

"What do we do now?" she asked.

"Wait," he replied, as his mind spun with possible plans of action but nothing came.

"How I long for the day when waiting isn't our only plan of inaction."

Kyle bristled from Maria's comment. He knew she meant nothing by it, but it still bothered him that he didn't know what to do. He couldn't think clearly. His mind was full of confusing, unclear images. *Not now,* he thought. *This is not the time for a flash.*

His fingers tapped against his leg for the first time that morning. This time, however, Kyle felt them pressing into his flesh and actually took notice of the action.

Tap, tap, tap. Tap, tap.

"I think I'm going to meditate for a while." He left the room, hoping to calm his mind before things got out of hand. They certainly didn't need two crises to deal with.

"Do you really think this is the right time to voluntarily make yourself unconscious?" Maria asked, following him into the living room. "You know, considering."

"I won't be unconscious," he explained, hoping he didn't sound condescending to the unenlightened. "Meditation allows me to perform a conscious exploration of my mind. It will give me the opportunity to organize my thoughts and purge any images that do not belong." Kyle often felt that people had a tendency to listen to him explain his beliefs as if they were humoring him because what he was saying was a joke somehow—especially his father. But he thought Maria of all people would understand. "Would you like to join me?"

"Thanks, but I like my cluttered mind the way it is," she said, although at the same time she took a few drops of her calming cedar oil.

Kyle took a seat on the floor, placing his body in the lotus position, with his legs crossed and folded over each other. He then closed his eyes and began his breathing exercises, trying to establish a sense of inner peace.

"Great, Michael's going to come back to find two unconscious bodies," Maria said to herself as she went back to Isabel's room.

Walking up to the bed to check on her friend, Maria's foot kicked something on the floor. Bending to retrieve the item, she found a copy of their yearbook lying there, closed. Maria picked it up, flipping through the pages and settling on the familiar photo of herself. Her face scrunched up as she once again regretted the awful picture. *What was I thinking?* she thought. *Talk about a bad hair day.*

Shutting the book so she no longer had to look at the offending picture, she placed it on Isabel's desk on top of another book that had been lying out. With nothing else to do, Maria sat by Isabel's side once again, holding her friend's hand and wondering what could be going on.

* * *

Isabel was banging against the door, frantically trying to break out of the room as if freedom from its confines would free her from Kyle's mind. Through the banging, she thought she had heard something on the other side. Putting her ear to the door, she listened and was able to make out faint voices, arguing. She assumed that it was just echoes of Tess and Alex.

The memory of his murder sent chills through her.

She almost yelled out for help before realizing how pointless that would have been since no one was really outside the door. Truth be told, she wasn't actually inside the room either, and it concerned her that her body was across town without a conscious mind inside. *Will I ever be able to get back?*

The voices disappeared, and Isabel gave up on the door entirely.

"Okay, Kyle." She turned back to the little boy. "Let's be proactive. You want me to stay here. Tell me why."

The six-year-old version of Kyle was throwing a baseball into the air and catching it as it came back down. "I don't know," he said as the ball went up into the air.

"Are you afraid of something?" She sat beside him on the bed, taking random guesses to try to figure out the problem.

The ball continued, up and down.

"Is it Tess?" she carefully pushed. "Are you afraid of Tess?"

The ball continued its repetitive journey.

"Is it someone else?" She tried a new track, with frustration creeping into her voice. "Did someone hurt you?"

Kyle missed the ball as it came down. It rolled across

the floor and under his dresser. The boy looked like he was about to tear up.

"I'll get it," Isabel offered. "Don't cry. It's just under the—"

"Big boys don't cry," he said firmly.

Hearing a response, she ignored the ball and focused on the boy. "And you're a big boy?"

"Yes," he said.

"But sometimes big boys *do* cry," she said. "If something really hurts—"

"No."

"Why do you say that?"

"Big boys don't cry."

"Okay, fine." Isabel gave up on trying to change his mind, and bent to the floor to get the ball. Reaching under the dresser, she slid her arm from left to right, but couldn't find it. The piece of furniture was small enough that she was able to touch the back wall, but she found nothing. The ball was gone. But, then again, it was never really there in the first place.

She thought about telling him that the ball was missing, but figured he probably knew, since this was his world and she was just a guest in it.

Giving up, she resumed her place beside little Kyle on the bed. "So are we going to sit here forever, or do you have something else in mind?"

Wordlessly, the boy finally got off the bed. Taking deliberate steps, he opened the bedroom door, waiting for her to follow.

Intrigued, she got up and went for the door. "So are you the ghost of Christmas past, present, or future?"

Little Kyle ignored her comment as they walked through the Valenti home and right into the police station. This time, however, it was empty. Making their way through a maze of twisting corridors that didn't exist in the real Roswell Police Station, Isabel followed the child right up to the sheriff's door.

He stopped there, waiting for her.

Assuming that it was her job to open the door, Isabel stepped up to turn the knob. "It's locked," she said after meeting resistance. Listening at the door, she had expected to hear someone crying again, but she heard nothing. "What is it, Kyle? What are you trying to tell me?"

"You're not supposed to go in there," he replied.

"Then why are we here?" She was trying to figure out this puzzle, but their trip was not a great example of linear thought. "What am I supposed to see?"

The world shifted around her as the fluorescents melted into the bright light of the sun, and the walls and floor fell away. They were back in the desert, at the same spot where Isabel had first entered into Kyle's nightmare. Little Kyle dropped to the ground and started digging.

The vulture or buzzard or whatever it was circled overhead while it either chased or was being chased by another one of its kind.

"What are you looking for?" Isabel asked, bending over the youngster and peering into the hole.

"Treasure," was his cryptic response.

"What kind of treasure?" She knelt beside him.

"Buried treasure."

Should have seen that one coming.

"Here, let me help." She dug into the ground with her

hands, thinking of the three-day-old manicure on her fingers as she clawed into the dirt with the pleasant knowledge that at least she was doing no real harm to her physical body. She figured that they would find whatever it was they were looking for much faster if she joined in. "How far do we have to dig?"

"Until we find what we're looking for," came yet another cryptic reply.

She could feel that something new had come into the dream.

Ignoring the digging for a moment, she saw an object glowing in the distance. Assuming that little Kyle would be okay on his own in his dream world, Isabel stood up and started walking to the strange object.

As she got closer, Isabel could see that it was some kind of huge iridescent orb hovering about three feet above the ground. Translucent colors swirled around the surface of the orb, and as Isabel approached it she could make out the shadow of an image inside.

She was so focused on the orb that she did not notice little Kyle had disappeared behind her and the birds were no longer in the sky above.

Stepping up to the strange sight, Isabel held her hand up to block the sun as she peered inside and saw the teenage version of Kyle that she was familiar with sitting in the center of the globe with his back to her. He was floating in what she recognized as the lotus position.

"Kyle!" she yelled, banging on the orb, wondering if this new version of her friend was there to answer some of her questions if only she could get through to him inside the sphere.

But he did not turn to her.

Assuming that he simply could not hear her while he was inside the orb, Isabel went around to face him. "Kyle!" She banged on the surface of the orb again while standing right in front of him.

His closed eyes did not open.

The orb began to radiate a bright light, replacing that of the now missing sun. Isabel stepped back as the orb expanded in size. For the first time, she noticed that parts of the desert image were disappearing, being replaced by blackness. Pieces of sky and earth had fallen away leaving nothingness behind as the place reorganized itself.

This is so not good, she thought as she began banging on the orb once again.

Energy flew from the orb, knocking her to the ground. A section of dirt disappeared beneath her hands as she nearly fell into the nothingness left in its place.

"Kyle!" She threw herself against the orb, fearing what would happen if she got trapped in the void that was enveloping the dream world. "Kyle!" She kicked at the expanding globe.

The darkness spread in pieces around her as Kyle was trying to organize his thoughts and remove the harmful imagery without realizing that he could be removing Isabel from existence. She had to take several steps to the left to keep from falling into the void as she saw the swirling colors of the sphere begin to fade. The surface of the orb began to clear, and she could see Kyle much more easily now, but his eyes were still closed to her. "Kyle!"

From within his meditative state, Kyle could hear a voice calling out to him. It was familiar to him. Using the techniques he had been self-taught, Kyle methodically tried to clear his mind, removing the offending images piece by piece as he reached out to the voice. More of the confusion fell away as he concentrated on the voice.

"Kyle, open your eyes!" she screamed. Knowing she had little time to act because the blackness was taking over, Isabel held out her hands and focused her concentration. She had no reason to believe that her alien powers would work in this dream world, but she was out of options.

Kyle heard Isabel that time. She was reaching out to him, calling for him. He tried to do whatever he could to answer her back.

Taking strength from her powerful fear, Isabel shot her hands out. Screaming Kyle's name, she forced the orb to burst in an explosion of light.

16

Michael pulled Kyle's car into an empty space right in front of Garrison's Hardware store and passed his hand over the dashboard to stop the engine. Double-checking to confirm that the sack he had previously picked up was tucked safely under the seat, he got out of the car.

Afraid to risk the important hidden items from being stolen, he fused the car locks with his hand. Now if anyone tried to break into the flashy car, they would have to do it by smashing the window or cutting through the cloth roof. *And let's assume the people strolling on the streets of Roswell would be Good Samaritans and stop the thief before he got in.*

Leaving the car behind, Michael went into Garrison's.

"Where do you keep your rope?" he asked, grabbing the first employee he saw as he stepped into the store.

Naturally, it was the *only* store employee, since the place was both owned and run by the somewhat Elderly Old Man Garrison. The nickname wasn't an insult, as the man wore it like a badge of honor, preferring to go by the title Elderly Old Man without believing the phrase to be even remotely redundant.

He was one of the oldest living residents of Roswell, and as such acted even older than his true age out of a desire to be treated like the oldest living resident in Roswell. It was rather unfortunate for Michael that Elderly Old Man Garrison was in one of his more eccentric moods when he woke up that morning and was apparently planning to stay that way for the rest of the day.

"What kind of rope?" Garrison asked.

"Rope," Michael said, wondering why he had even bothered to ask. The place was one of the smaller stores on Roswell's main drag. It wasn't like it would have taken him hours to find the item he was looking for on his own.

"Well, what do you want to do with the rope?" Elderly Old Man Garrison asked. "Different kinds of jobs take different kinds of ropes."

"Right now, I'm thinking of a hanging," Michael suggested.

Elderly Old Man Garrison's laughter turned into a wheezing attack. Granted, he wasn't actually having a real breathing problem, it was all just part of the act.

I hate these quaint colorful small-town characters, Michael thought. *Why couldn't ours have been the set of pods that was transported to New York? At least there the crazies are actually crazy.*

Garrison recovered from his false asthma attack and set into his routine. "Now, for small jobs, you can use some twine or maybe even some fishing line. Fishing line is good because it's strong but lightweight. Now, we don't actually carry fishing line, but we do have twine—"

"Listen, Old Man—"

"That's *Elderly* Old Man, sonny." He was having the most fun he had had in a long time. His favorite playmates were the kids who never seemed to have any interest in playing along.

Michael lamented the fact that he had not brought Maria along, because she was much better suited to handle these types of characters. *In many ways, she is one of these types of characters,* he thought.

"Sir," Michael stressed the word, which apparently impressed the Elderly Old Man. "I'm in a bit of a hurry, so please either tell me where the rope is or I will have to take my business elsewhere."

Never one to let his fun get in the way of turning a profit, Garrison pointed Michael in the right direction. "Aisle three, sonny. And you let me know if you need any help."

"Sure," Michael said, having absolutely no intention to ask even if he had to climb the shelves himself to reach what he was looking for.

Hurrying down aisle three, Michael found a huge collection of rope of all different varieties. *Good thing I cut the old man off,* he thought, *or we'd be here all afternoon.*

Grabbing a bag of fifty-foot-long, one-inch-wide rope off the shelf, Michael hurried back to make his purchase. He had taken too much time in getting the first items on his list and he could already hear Maria complaining about his disappearance. He didn't need to take any longer.

For once the delay wasn't Michael's fault. *If Kyle could learn to fill his car with gas once in a while,* he cursed his friend one more time. Michael had considered just driving along without any gas in the car. It was possible to do that with his powers, but it didn't really do nice things to the engine. Instead, Michael had to use his powers to push the car to a gas station for a fill-up.

Luckily, he only had one more stop on the list before he could head back to Isabel's side. Of course, he still had to have another run-in with Elderly Old Man Garrison at the checkout.

"Found that rope?" Elderly asked the obvious as Michael dropped his purchase on the counter in front of him.

"Yes." Michael decided to keep his answers short and sweet.

Apparently where money was concerned, Elderly Old Man Garrison was just as happy to keep the transaction quick and efficient, and Michael easily paid for the items and rushed out of the store.

"Come back soon," the store owner hollered with a wave.

Ignoring the man, Michael continued walking down the Roswell main shopping district to a store called The Pottery Place. The store window was full of more knick-knacks and dust collectors than he ever imagined anyone could possibly need. Quite frankly, he had never expected to see the inside of the store in his lifetime in Roswell, but he had certainly done stranger things in the unending quest to combat strange alien phenomena.

Bracing himself for the smell of potpourri and the sounds of wind chimes, Michael entered the curiosity shop. *The things I do for my friends,* was the last thing he thought before the kitsch overwhelmed him.

* * *

If Michael had taken just a few more seconds to prepare himself before entering the store, he would have run into Jim Valenti coming out of Moby Disc, the music store attached to The Pottery Place. Valenti was carrying a bag full of sheet music and a hastily purchased guitar, still humming the same happy tune that had been stuck in his head all day.

Loading the items into his SUV, Valenti checked to confirm that his earlier purchases were still on the front seat, then pulled out onto the street. He drove his car through town, passing the Evanses' home, entirely unaware of the drama going on inside involving his son and his friends. Continuing several blocks over, he pulled up in front of a house with the garage wide open.

As he got out of his SUV, Valenti heard familiar music coming from the garage that, not so coincidentally, happened to be the very same tune he had been humming for the better part of the morning. *Good, they started without me,* he thought as he pulled his bags and his new guitar out of the vehicle.

From the open garage, the band saw him walking up the drive and stopped playing their song. The three remaining members of the group formerly known as The Whits looked at one another with a growing sense of anticipation.

"Sorry I'm late, fellas." Valenti entered the garage, carefully setting down his guitar. "I rode out to a music store in Hondo first thing this morning. Had to pick up some sheet music I'd special ordered. There are some really great rockabilly tunes in here." He held up one of his bags.

"Rockabilly?" the drummer, Chris, sounded skeptical.

"We're really more of an alternative band," Marcus, the rhythm guy, added. "Kind of a younger sound." He had stressed the word *younger* when he said it.

"I know, I know," Valenti said. "But you have to try these songs. I promise you, it will be a great new sound for us."

Chris and Marcus looked to their new leader, Mickey, silently willing him to have the conversation they had previously talked about that morning. Being trained in detective work, Valenti caught the glares and started putting things together. It wasn't a difficult case to crack.

"Is something wrong, Mickey?" he asked.

"Can you guys give us a second?" the lead guitarist asked his other band members.

Without another word, Chris and Marcus fled the garage.

"Let me guess." Valenti saved the teen from the difficult job he had been left to do. "It's not working out."

"Look, Sheriff—"

"Jim," he corrected the boy. "I haven't been a sheriff for over five months now."

Mickey was uncomfortable calling him by his first name. "Mr. Valenti, the guys and I have been having a great time the past few days. I mean, all the jamming we've been doing has really been fun."

"But starting a band with someone my age doesn't fit into your plans," Valenti finished the thought for him, hoping to save the boy from the embarrassment of having to say it to him.

"That's not it." Mickey sat on the ratty old couch that

his parents had thrown into the garage for him and his friends. An unnoticed plume of dust rose from the cushion. "The whole band thing isn't really in our plans. You see, Alex was really the driving force behind The Whits."

"I know." Valenti thought about Alex. "It was the one part of his life where he really came out of his shell."

"And without him, there is no band," Mickey added. "When you came up to us at the memorial, we were all excited to have the chance to go on with the group, but—"

"It's not the same," he guessed.

"Not really," the teen admitted. "It has nothing to do with you. It's just that none of us is all that interested anymore. With senior year approaching and colleges to look at—"

"No, no, I understand. And I've got to tell you, Mickey, it takes a good man to know what he wants in life and not be afraid to say it."

"Thanks, sir," Mickey replied, getting off the old couch.

"Please, knock off the sir stuff."

"Okay . . . Jim." He held out his hand for Valenti to shake. "Kyle's really lucky to have an understanding father like you."

"Thanks." Valenti beamed at the compliment. "But about Kyle . . . can you and the guys keep this whole band thing just between us? I think it would embarrass him to know that his dad's been hanging out with his classmates."

"It'll be our secret."

"See you around," Valenti said, grabbing his guitar and making his way out of the garage. As he walked down the drive, he nodded his good-bye to the other band members who were hanging out on the porch. They waved and smiled in response. *Roswell's got some good kids in it,* he thought.

Back in his SUV, Valenti paused after placing the key in the ignition. Singing with the band had been the first recreational thing he had done in months, and he was going to miss it. It was nice to take a break from the responsibilities inherent in his more "alien" endeavors. He did understand where the kids were coming from, but that didn't necessarily mean that he couldn't continue with his plans.

Starting up the engine, Valenti's mind started working on an idea. He looked over to the passenger seat and saw the bags full of sheet music he had spent the morning collecting. *It would be a shame to let all that music go to waste,* he thought as he pulled away from the curb. *And maybe it is time I started doing things with people my own age. I do tend to spend most of my time with friends who are young enough to be my children.*

Valenti turned the idea over in his head for the rest of his drive home. Music had always been an important part of his life in the past. In fact, there had been a time while he was in high school when it was even more important to him than going into law enforcement. Now that he was no longer sheriff, he considered that it could be time again to give music another try. All he would need to do is gather up a band . . . and maybe come up with a really good name for the group.

Feeling more motivated than he had since losing his job, Valenti started putting together his plans. He thought of some guys he could get in contact with who he knew liked to play. He also thought of a few local bars that were always looking to showcase new talent. All they would really need was a place to rehearse, preferably outside of his own home so that he wouldn't have to tell Kyle until he was sure it was going to work out. The rest of the ride, he continued to build on his ideas for the band that would eventually become known as the Kit-Shickers.

17

Liz shuffled through the magazines in the doctor's outer office, lamenting the fact that everything had a published date of at least a year ago. She was looking for something to take her mind off her concerns for Jason as he was being examined in the other room. *He has to be okay. It's just a little bruise.* But she couldn't help think of the bigger wounds that they couldn't see.

She should have realized that the changes in Jason had been caused by something serious, since he had totally shut her out. It was one thing for him to break away from his parents, since that was traditionally part of the process of growing up, but for him to shut himself off from a close, trusted friend was a real sign of trouble.

Liz blamed herself. Her own world had turned so crazy since Max had saved her life that day in the Crashdown that it was understandable she might have missed the warning signs. She could have been around more, considering Artesia had gotten a lot closer once she had obtained her driver's license. But she knew that the real person to blame was George Lyles, and she would certainly have the time to deal with that.

Frustrated, she dropped the copies of out-of-date *Time* and *Newsweek* magazines back into the rack and settled on an old copy of *Highlights* magazine for children. Turning to the puzzle section, she intended to test her mind with harmless, easy-to-solve riddles as opposed to the difficult games she seemed to be stuck with every day lately.

"This isn't the first bruise like this I've seen on you," Dr. Sellers said as he examined Jason's shoulder.

As usual, Jason said nothing, sitting on the examination table staring down at his feet. Max noticed that he had shut down once again as soon as they had reached Dr. Sellers's doorstep.

"I guess he's an active kid," Max offered, not quite sure how much to say right then.

They had been lucky enough to find Jason's family doctor at home that Saturday. The affable older man was kind enough to open the office attached to his home to give Jason the once-over. Liz and Max explained that he had fallen off his ATV after having gone on a little unsupervised joyride, assuming that it would be best not to raise questions about why the two teens had let him go out on his bike without his parents around.

"I'm sorry, how was it that you know Jason?" the doctor asked, genuinely concerned for the child's safety. Max gave the man extra points for being so obviously protective.

"He's my friend." Jason offered the first kind words to Max since they had met yesterday speaking through his locked bedroom door.

"He and Liz grew up together," Max added, since Liz had decided to stay out in the waiting room to give Jason some privacy. "In Roswell."

"Okay," the doctor said both to the explanation and to indicate he was done with the examination. "You can put your shirt back on. Everything looks fine to me, but I'll want you to come back with your mom on Monday so we can get some X rays just to be sure."

Jason nodded his head.

"We'll make sure he comes back," Max added.

"Good," Dr. Sellers replied. "Jason, do you mind if I speak to Max for a moment?"

Jason looked to Max to see if it was okay.

"Why don't you go out and wait with Liz," Max said as the boy hopped down off the table. "I'm sure I'll only be a minute."

"Okay," Jason said softly as he left the room.

Once the boy was out of earshot, the doctor turned to Max. "I don't know exactly how close you two are, but Jason seems to trust you."

"I hope," Max said.

The doctor continued. "Jason hasn't really trusted anyone for a while now."

Max was confused at just how closely the doctor knew his patient, and apparently his face showed his bewilderment.

"It's a small town," Sellers explained. "People come to me with their medical problems and they open up about other things too. His mom's a good woman."

"She seems to be," Max agreed. "I know she and Liz are very close."

"Like I said, I've noticed these bruises before," the doctor continued. "I never really put it together."

"We're taking care of it," Max assured him. "Jason's opening up to us. We're going to talk to his mom."

"I'm glad to hear that," the doctor said. "He's a good kid. You did the right thing bringing him here."

Max was pleased by the doctor's words. It was the first sign that he was doing the right thing in his role as guardian for the weekend. "Thanks."

"Take my card." The doctor handed him a small slip of paper. "Please call me no matter what happens."

"Okay." Max shook the doctor's hand.

He went out into the lobby and collected Liz and Jason, bolstered by the doctor's simple words. For the first time that weekend, he felt like he was in control. They had resolved Jason's attitude problems and were going to tackle the larger issue when his parents returned. Not only that, but also had an adult on their side who happened to be a medical expert. This bolstered Max's confidence to believe that everything would turn out right.

"Jason said everything was fine?" Liz confirmed as they walked back out to the bikes. They had been so concerned about getting Jason checked out immediately that neither of them had even thought to stop back at the house and pick up Max's car.

"Looks that way," Max replied. "Dr. Sellers wants him to come in Monday for some X rays."

They could both see the look of trepidation on Jason's face as he climbed aboard the ATV behind Max.

"I'll go too," Liz offered. "I can stay until Monday."

"Are you sure?" Jason asked.

"I'll stay as long as you need me," she replied.

They rode the bikes back to Jason's home, carefully sticking to the road so as not to risk any more adventures. Max wasn't sure if ATVs were okay to ride on the street, but he honestly didn't care. It was only a short trip from the doctor's place, and they found themselves pulling back into the garage only a few minutes later. Placing the two remaining sets of keys on the rack, they made their way to the house.

Entering the Lyleses' foyer, the trio split into different directions. Jason went upstairs to change, since his clothes were torn and dirty from the fall. Max's clothes were a bit dusty as well, but hunger was his primary distraction, since he was the only one of them who had left the house without breakfast. He hadn't had a shower, either, but that could wait until his stomach stopped grumbling. Making his way to the kitchen, he left Liz to check the answering machine to see if Jason's parents had called while they were out.

Searching through the kitchen cabinets hoping for something to ease his hunger, Max was hopeful when he found a bottle of Tabasco sauce. Now he just needed something to pour it over. In the adjoining cabinet, he found what he was looking for in one of those incredibly sugary breakfast bars. True, it wasn't a lot of food, but it would hold him over until they could put together something for lunch. Pouring the Tabasco over the breakfast bar for just the right sweet and spicy snack, he had taken only one bite when Liz called to him from the living room. The tone of her voice implied that he should hurry.

"What's wrong?" he asked as soon as he entered the room with his breakfast bar still in hand.

"Listen to this," she replied, pressing the "play" button on the machine.

The machine announced that there were four messages, and after a short pause, Maria's voice came through. "Liz. Max. Where are you? You guys need to get back here, fast. Something's wrong with Isabel. She's sick. We think it's some kind of Czechoslovakian flu. Hurry."

Max blanched.

A drop of Tabasco sauce fell onto the spotless beige carpet.

He knew that *Czechoslovakian* was Liz's and Maria's code word for anything alien related. Something was seriously wrong with his sister, and it sounded like Maria didn't have a clue what it was.

"The other messages are from Maria too." Liz stopped the tape so Max would not hear the increasing desperation in Maria's voice with each call. "She said she's at your place. Give her a call, and I'll go get Jason."

"We can't take him to Roswell," Max said as he took the phone from Liz.

"Well, we can't leave him here," Liz said. "And I'm not staying behind if something is really wrong with your sister."

"It could be dangerous," he said, dialing his own phone number.

"If things turn out to be too intense, we'll drop him off with my folks," Liz said as she left the room, ending the argument right there.

"Evans residence," Maria answered on the other end of the line.

"It's me," Max said. "What's wrong?"

Maria filled him in on the situation, which didn't take long since she couldn't tell him much. Following a litany of questions that she couldn't answer, Max finally gave up on asking for information that she obviously did not possess. He turned to see Liz and Jason standing in the doorway, ready to travel. "We'll be there in twenty minutes," he said into the phone.

"But you're over forty miles away," Maria answered back.

"We'll be there," he insisted, hanging up the phone. "Jason, how do you feel about visiting your old hometown?"

Kyle's eyes popped open.

He had been prematurely forced out of his meditation when he heard Isabel calling his name. Running to the bedroom, he found Maria cradling the phone in her hands with an expression of relief across her face.

"Max and Liz are on their way," she reported, looking at her watch to see that it was already one o'clock in the afternoon. She had no idea if their friends could do anything more than she and Kyle were already doing, but the mere fact that they were on their way back was comforting. For Max to be there in twenty minutes meant he would have to break more than a few traffic laws. Hopefully, former Sheriff Valenti could take care of it if anything happened.

"I think Isabel tried to contact me," Kyle said.

"What? How?"

"When I was meditating," he explained. "I was in the process of purging my mind when I saw her for a brief moment. She was calling my name."

"Did she tell you how we can help her?" Maria asked the obvious.

"No," Kyle said as he took a seat beside his comatose friend. "But she seemed desperate. I don't think we have much time."

"Don't worry, I've got a plan," Michael said as he climbed in the window and dropped a large sack on the floor.

Kyle was up and around the bed beside Maria in a matter of moments, watching as Michael first took a collection of stones from his sack. Maria instantly recognized them, but Kyle had no clue as to what good they would be.

"I figure if anything's going to help us it's these," Michael said with his usual intensity. Then, looking at Kyle, he explained further. "Before you were brought into our ever expanding inner circle, a Native American guy named River Dog gave us these. I took part in one of his rituals, and it nearly killed me. These stones come from our home planet. They saved me."

Maria was visibly upset at the reminder of the time when she had almost lost Michael, but she tried not to dwell on it because it was in the past, and in the present there was a more pressing threat. "Max is on his way."

"We need to prepare." Michael returned to his magic sack and pulled out the long rope, handing it to Maria. "I need you to cut five pieces of rope that are about four feet long."

"Okay?" she said with a question in her voice. "What do you want me to do with the rest?"

"Bring it back with the smaller pieces."

"Gotcha." She was out of the room in a flash to search for something she could use to cut the thick rope.

"Kyle, help me out," Michael said, moving to the bed, motioning for Kyle to get on the other side.

Grabbing one side of the headboard, he instructed Kyle to do the same. Together, they slid Isabel and her bed about two feet away from the wall so it was closer to the center of the room. "Maria!" Michael called out into the hall.

"Almost done!" she yelled back.

Tension filled the air as Michael impatiently waited for his girlfriend to return. Kyle knew better than to say anything when Michael was in this kind of mood. He would only throw rude comments back.

"What exactly are we doing?" Maria asked, coming back into the room. She apparently was used to the rude comments.

"Making a medicine wheel," Michael stated simply as he took the longer piece of rope from her. Walking around the bed, he laid the rope on the floor in a circle. It was a little long, so the ends overlapped for a good three feet.

That task complete, Michael held his hand out to Maria, and she handed him the smaller pieces she had cut with a kitchen knife. "I didn't have the time to collect a few hundred rocks to make the same design River Dog made when I was sick. We'll have to go with this." He started laying out the rope one piece at a time, leaving one end beside Isabel with the other end on the rope circle.

The plan was to use the rope to re-create the medicine wheel design that River Dog had laid out on the ground when Michael's friends had had to pull him back from his own near death experience. When placing the smaller ropes beside Isabel on the bed, he had to cheat a little since a couple of the pieces weren't long enough to reach from her to the circle on the floor. However, he really didn't think it mattered, because the design probably had nothing to do with the healing.

The Royal Four had used the healing stones twice since then to revive Nasedo—although only one of the attempts had been successful. They hadn't re-created the medicine wheel design on those occasions, but with Isabel's life at stake, Michael wasn't taking any chances. He looked down at the five lines radiating out from Isabel to equidistant points around the circle. It wasn't exactly pretty, nor was it entirely complete with several gaps throughout, but it would have to do.

Michael went back to his goody bag and pulled out the last item. It was a bowl he had bought in The Pottery Place that was painted with some kind of Native American "inspired" artwork. He actually suspected that it was just a cheap tourist knockoff. It still had a price tag glued to the side, which he quickly rubbed off. "Fill this with water." He handed it to Kyle. "And we'll be ready as soon as Max and Liz arrive."

The darkness receded, and the desert flew back into place.

Isabel took a moment to reorient herself after nearly losing touch with the fictional reality in which she was trapped. Kyle and the mysterious orb had disappeared as curiously as they had appeared. For a brief moment she had seen him with his eyes open and had noticed the shock on his face as if he wasn't expecting to see her.

She wondered if it was just a dream image of Kyle or if

maybe her friends were trying to rescue her. She had hoped the latter was the case, but couldn't stop thinking about the fact that her entire family was gone for the weekend. It was very possible that no one would be aware of what she was going through until late Sunday night, and she worried that could be too late.

Making her way back to the spot where she had been digging, she thought that little Kyle had disappeared as well. But as she got closer, she realized that the hole was now deep enough that little Kyle could bend down in it and be totally hidden from view. Isabel sensed that they were never going to find what they were looking for until Kyle's subconscious allowed them to, and she didn't see that happening anytime in the near future.

"You stopped digging," the boy said when she returned to him.

"You intend to keep us digging forever," she simply replied.

He looked guilty at having been caught.

"Look, Kyle, I came here to help, but you're not letting me," Isabel said gently. "If you insist on keeping me here, you're going to have to give me some more to work with."

The pair of buzzards—or vultures—was circling again. Strangely, Isabel took this as a good sign. A road appeared, knifing through the desert, with a car parked alongside it. The car looked to be from the eighties, but Isabel really knew nothing about cars.

Laughter filled the air.

Great. More imagery. And me without my dream analysis book. Well, at least it's something.

The birds seemed to be talking to each other, letting out

caws that at first sounded cheerful but evolved into angry bellows. The sounds grew louder as Isabel had to struggle to hear her own thoughts.

The laughter either stopped or was drowned out by the screeching birds.

Kyle looked very, very afraid.

"It's okay," she said loudly while comforting the child. "I'm here."

"But you'll go away," he said.

"I might leave your mind," she replied, not wanting to lie to him, "but I promise I will never leave you."

At that moment the birds attacked each other as their lazy circles grew into fierce battle. Isabel could only watch, hoping that the fight did not come any closer as their caws got even louder.

One of the birds abruptly disappeared, leaving the other alone in flight. The lone bird landed next to Isabel and Kyle, but made no threatening moves toward them. It appeared to be injured, cradling its wing.

The sounds of screeches echoed away and were replaced by the sound of crying. It was the same sound she had heard coming from behind the door to the sheriff's office when she had been there earlier. This time, Isabel could tell that it was definitely a man's sobs and, if she wasn't mistaken, she recognized the choked voice of the man between his deep intakes of breath.

Again, she looked at the wounded bird. *Was it doing the crying?*

Without having to consult her book on dream imagery, Isabel finally had enough pieces of the puzzle to begin to understand what all this was about. Unfortunately, as she watched the bird, she hadn't noticed that little Kyle had disappeared.

Running back to the hole, she saw something peeking up through the dirt. She fell to the ground, pushing the dirt out of the way to find Alex's face staring back at her. He was buried beneath the desert. His dead eyes were locked on her.

Isabel recoiled in shock.

It took her a minute to recover.

The pieces are beginning to tie together, she realized, *but what am I supposed to do now?*

18

Upon hearing the screeching tires of Max's car as it pulled up to the house, Michael ran out of Isabel's room. Running through the house, he had the front door open and he was at the ready to greet his friend and leader.

Pushing past the second in command, Max burst into his home and made a beeline for his sister's room without so much as a "hello." Liz followed, trying to ease Jason's concerns without actually telling him why Max was in such an agitated state, which was difficult to do since they had just traveled north on 285 at double the maximum speed allowed by law.

"Who's the kid?" Michael asked in his typical gruff and unwelcoming manner.

"Who's the dork?" the kid shot back.

Michael smiled. "I like him," he said, and went to take his preordained place by Max's side without waiting for a formal introduction.

Not knowing what they would find in Isabel's room, Liz told Jason to stay in the living room and distracted him

with the TV and the Evanses' video collection. Remembering that he wasn't the little boy she used to know, Liz
avoided suggesting the Disney classics in place of something he'd rather be seeing. Eventually, she just let him
pick a film himself since she knew there was nothing in
the collection that was too mature for his viewing. She
warned him to stay where he was no matter what he
heard, explaining that Isabel could be contagious and she
didn't want him getting sick too. It was a little white lie,
but partially true since honestly she didn't want him
exposed to whatever could be happening in the other
room. Once he agreed, Liz went to join her friends.

In Isabel's room, Max went straight to his sister's side,
hardly bothering to notice his friends or the changes in the
room's design. Taking Isabel's hand, he did the same check
for fever, pulse, and breath rate as everyone else who had
entered the room had immediately done. Like the others,
he found nothing out of the ordinary—except that his sister still appeared to be in a coma.

With his hand still on her forehead, he closed his eyes
and tried to make contact with her. He hoped that his
healing power alone would be enough to save her, but he
got no response. It was almost as if her mind was not in
there to answer him back.

He reluctantly took his hand away, silently blaming
himself for everything from having gone away for the
weekend to being the reason they were stranded on Earth.
Self-recrimination was always his first thought when anything happened to his family or friends.

"Uneasy lies the head that wears the crown."

It was that line from Shakespeare's *Henry IV, Part 2* that

often came to Max's mind in situations like these. He had never actually read the play, but he was familiar enough with the quote that he had heard one day in English class. Ever since he had found out that he was literally the king of his home planet he had truly come to understand its meaning.

And now I want to bring a child up in this mess, he thought, once again doubting his own abilities even though his apparent weekend success story was in the living room watching television.

"What happened to you?" Maria broke through his thoughts, referring to the dirty state of his still unchanged clothes.

"Long story," he replied.

Turning to Michael, Max's expression asked what to do next.

"Everyone take a point along the circle," Michael said, accepting the mantle of command. He passed out a stone to each of his friends as they filed into place, holding one for Liz until she came into the room. "Remember, all of our thoughts need to be with Isabel to bring her back."

Kyle was the only one of the group unfamiliar with the ritual, since he had not taken part in it when Michael had been ill. That was back when Kyle was still considered one of the "bad guys," when, in truth, he had only been an innocent bystander. "What is it exactly that we're doing?" he asked, examining the stone that was placed in his hand.

"Restoring the balance," Michael abruptly replied.

"Oh." Kyle was still totally unclear. "Okay."

"Cliff's Notes version," Maria built on her boyfriend's non-answer. "Michael thinks there's something wrong with the energy in Isabel's body. The stones carry the same energy. We concentrate on Isabel. We're taken to some higher plane of existence where we get her and bring her back."

"Higher plane of existence?" He worried if where they were going was sanctioned by Buddha.

"Just concentrate on Isabel and you'll get back fine," she replied. "I hope."

Kyle tried to ignore her last comment as Liz came into the room, immediately realized what was happening, and took her place on the empty spot along the medicine wheel.

Michael handed Liz the last remaining healing stone and picked up the bowl. River Dog had claimed that water was a substance the aliens and humans had in common and was used to bond them in the ritual. Taking a sip, he then handed the bowl to Max on his left. Max also took a drink from the bowl and passed it to Kyle, who went along with the ritual by passing it to Liz. The bowl finally ended with Maria, who placed it on the nightstand beside her, leaving a few sips of water in the bowl, figuring they might need it for Isabel when they revived her.

Now came the hardest part. River Dog had taught them all a chant to accompany the ritual. Although the phrase had been responsible for saving his life and thus the sound of it was permanently emblazoned into his mind, Michael was not familiar enough with the Native American language to know the exact words or their meaning. Sounding the words out carefully, he began the chant, hoping the pronunciation came close enough to the correct phrase. *"Taa-KAH-shalah BEY-ta-wa ah-JAH . . ."*

He indicated to the others that they should join in, hoping it was their joined concentration behind the words that had mattered more than the words themselves, which he knew he was butchering by even attempting to recite them without a proper translator available.

"Taa-KAH-shalah BEY-ta-wa ah-JAH . . ."

"Taa-KAH-shalah BEY-ta-wa ah-JAH . . ."

"Taa-KAH-shalah BEY-ta-wa ah-JAH . . ."

They continued the chant, each reaching out to Isabel separately and together as one. With eyes closed, they tried to find their friend, restore the balance, and bring her back. Intensity crept into their voices as they continued to search for their lost member, without any response. But instead of images of Isabel, each of them only saw the darkness behind their sealed eyes.

Max realized it had not taken anywhere near this long to locate Michael when he was ill. Peering out, he looked down to his sister and saw no change in her prone body. *"Taa-KAH-shalah BEY-ta-wa ah-JAH,"* he said even louder, willing the others to match him in both volume and force. He did not care that Jason was in the other room and could probably hear them. His sister's life could be at stake, and worrying about the possible discovery of their alien secret by a twelve-year-old was not high on his priority scale.

"Taa-KAH-shalah BEY-ta-wa ah-JAH . . ."

"Max," he heard Michael's voice, but ignored it.

"Taa-KAH-shalah BEY-ta-wa ah-JAH," he repeated the chant again, knowing that he was the only one in the room still speaking.

"Max, it's not working," Michael gently insisted as Max

felt the people on either side of him already moving away from the circle.

Opening his eyes, Max confirmed that all of his friends already had a look of resignation on their faces.

"Maybe we did need to use a circle of rocks. . . . I could find River Dog," Michael suggested. "If we knew the exact words . . ."

"No," Max said. "It won't work."

"It was just a guess," Liz quickly went the positive route. "There's probably a lot more we can try."

But Max barely heard her as he moved in to protective mode. "Kyle, was Isabel like this when you found her?"

"Actually, she was sitting up," he explained. "In a very uncomfortable-looking position. I laid her down."

"What was the room like?" Max continued. "Was anything out of place?"

"No," Kyle admitted. "It pretty much looked the same way it does now, except for the bed and rope. Oh, and I borrowed your baseball bat. Hope you don't mind."

Maria flashed him a confused look.

"And you didn't move anything else?" Max asked, ignoring the last part.

"Actually," Maria chimed in, "I did find her yearbook on the floor. I put it on the desk."

Both Max's and Michael's faces lit up at the clue, although no one else in the room knew the significance of the yearbook.

"Why didn't you say anything?" Michael asked in an accusing tone.

Before Maria had a chance to express her confusion, Max cleared things up for her and the rest of their friends. "Isabel uses her yearbook when she dreamwalks on our class-mates." He bent over his sister and noticed that her eyelids were fluttering slightly. Max knew that this was a result of the rapid eye movements experienced when people dream. "Was it open to a specific page when you found it?"

"No. It was closed," Maria replied, picking up the book and seeing the one beneath it. "Look at this. A book on dream analysis."

"Okay, we know what's going on. Now we just have to figure out who she was dreamwalking—," Max said.

"No, we don't," Kyle interrupted. "It's me."

Kyle proceeded to explain his previous request that Isabel help fix his dreams and the reason why he had asked. He detailed every bit of his sleeping problem and his conversations with Isabel.

"Why didn't you say something sooner?" Michael said in his normal accusatory way.

"She said she wasn't going to do it because it was too dangerous," Kyle replied defensively. "It never occurred to me that she would try it without telling anyone."

"She does have a tendency to act on her own," Max said. "And I've never known her to back down when a friend's life could be at stake."

"Wait a minute." Kyle froze. "I just want to be clear on this. Are you saying Isabel's currently trapped in my mind?"

Max's face was stone as he nodded.

"Well, get her out!" Kyle yelled.

Hoping to break the tension, Maria walked up to him and yelled in his ear, "Don't worry, Isabel. We're working on it!"

The joke didn't go over very well. The tension remained, though there was now a loud ringing in Kyle's ear to distract him for a moment.

"Has something like this ever happened when she dreamwalked before?" Liz asked.

"Never," Max replied. "I have no clue how to stop it. Michael and I can't consciously enter a person's mind like that."

"Are you sure?" Maria asked, not wanting to broach a sensitive subject. "Michael and Isabel do have that connection. You know, from before they were sent here."

Maria was, quite reluctantly, bringing up the topic of the former relationship between Michael and Isabel when they were on their home planet. The two had shared some mental links in their human form, most notably when Isabel thought he had impregnated her in her dreams.

"Maybe Michael should try to reach her," Maria suggested.

"I don't think so," Liz interjected. "She's in Kyle's mind. He's probably the only one who could get through to her."

"I did see her earlier when I meditated," Kyle suggested. "But as soon as I realized she was there, I was pushed right out of my trance."

"You need to reach out through your mind," Liz replied.

"How?" Kyle asked. "Last time I checked, I was a mere mortal—well, mostly mortal."

"Through your dreams," she explained. "You need to go back to sleep."

"In case you missed what I said earlier," he replied, "I haven't been having the easiest time falling asleep lately. How do you suggest we do this?"

"Ooh, hang on." Maria bounced over to her purse and started digging around, finally pulling out a small bottle that she handed to Kyle. "Use this."

Kyle looked at it skeptically.

"It's a relaxation aid," she explained. "Purely natural ingredients, nothing to worry about."

"I don't know." He was still reluctant. "Sleeping pills?"

"No," she said. "Not sleeping pills. They're just some herbs that help with relaxation. I use them at particularly stressful times in my life when the cedar oil I usually rely on isn't relaxing enough. You know, like when our lives are in some sort of mortal peril, or the night before a really big test."

Kyle looked at Isabel, still lying motionless on her bed. He felt a tremendous amount of guilt over the fact that everything appeared to be his fault. *But why did you try to help me on your own?* "And you're sure it's safe?" he asked.

"My mom wouldn't let me take it if she hadn't totally checked it out." Maria looked absolutely sure of herself.

Hesitant, Kyle took one of the herbal capsules out of the bottle, staring at it as if it were dangerous. The blue capsule looked harmless enough to Kyle, but so did Michael, and he could kill people with his thoughts.

"Here, take it with this." Maria lifted the bowl off the nightstand. It still had some water left in it from their failed ritual.

"This has been one strange day." Kyle swallowed the capsule in a gulp.

As Michael and Maria carefully returned Isabel's room to its normal setup, Max took Kyle to his room to give him a comfortable bed to lie in and relax. Liz followed, covering the windows and dimming the lights for him. Once everything was set up and Kyle was comfortably in bed, Michael and Maria joined them.

"Is everything okay?" Max asked.

"I can't decide if the bed is too hard, too soft, or just right," Kyle replied. "Do you have any porridge?"

No one laughed at the truly lame joke.

"Are you tired?" Max asked. "Do you think you can fall asleep?"

"It would probably be easier if I didn't have four people staring intensely at me," Kyle said.

Max immediately understood. "I should go check on Jason."

"Yeah, we'll go too," Maria agreed as they all started to leave the room.

"Liz." Kyle stopped his ex-girlfriend. "Would you mind staying?"

Instinctively, she looked to Max for approval or to apologize for her connection to Kyle, but Max consciously chose not to return her glance. With his sister's life in jeopardy, this was not the time for petty jealousies. Besides, he had been trying to move beyond her bond with Kyle just as he hoped that she could move past his relationship with Tess.

After the others filed out of the room, Liz sat beside Kyle on Max's bed and took his hand into hers. It was certainly an odd situation, no matter how one looked at it, and they both couldn't help but smile.

"So, back when we were dating," Kyle said, heading for dangerous territory, "did you ever think we'd end up like this?"

"What? Didn't you?" Liz played along. "Lying in my

new boyfriend's bed while you tried to release his sister who is trapped in your dreams? I always suspected that our relationship would end when I met an alien and threw all of our lives into almost constant peril."

"Yeah, me too," Kyle agreed sleepily. "I just wanted to make sure we both had had the same expectations."

"Maria's magical herbs seem to be working?" Liz asked hopefully.

Kyle stifled a yawn in response. "How do you think I'm supposed to find Isabel once I'm asleep?"

"Honestly?" Liz said. "I have no idea. It's not exactly like we're treading on scientifically proven ground here. But, I can't think of anything else we could do."

"Is it worth it?" Kyle turned serious for a moment. "All that we've been through? All that we're going to be put through?"

Liz thought about his question. There was no easy answer. "I don't know. Obviously, in light of Alex, I'd have to say no. But then I think about Max, Michael, and Isabel going through all of this by themselves with no one to turn to for help and I have to be glad that we can be there for them."

"In spite of getting shot, running from the FBI, and Isabel getting trapped in my brain?" Kyle added with a full yawn.

"Yeah, in spite of all that." Liz smiled. "Maybe we should stop talking so you can get some rest."

"Okay," he said sleepily, closing his eyes. "Good night, Liz."

"Good night," she replied.

Liz stayed with Kyle, listening to his breathing grow more steady. It did not take long for him to fall into what she had hoped would be a productive sleep. She waited a few minutes to confirm that he was definitely out before moving over to the chair by Max's desk. She had no intention of leaving him alone while he experienced whatever it was he was about to go through.

Watching over his sleeping form, she wished Kyle luck on his journey, hoping he would be able to rescue Isabel and gain whatever kind of closure he needed to end his own suffering.

19

Kyle stood in the middle of his living room.

Alone.

"Isabel?" he yelled. "Isabel, are you here?"

But no answer came.

Then, he heard the familiar voices, fighting . . . scream-ing . . . dying.

He made his way over to his bedroom door. He had hoped he would never have to witness this event again. It was the same hope he'd had every time he'd closed his eyes the past few weeks. But he knew he would have to go where the dream took him if he was to find Isabel and free her from his mind. If only he knew how he was expected to do that.

Placing his hand on the knob, he couldn't bring himself to turn it. The metal felt warm to the touch and was grow-ing hotter. *Do it for Isabel,* he thought, and flung the door open without further hesitation.

This time, however, he did not see a frightened Tess and a battered Alex. This time, his room was as empty as the living room. Although if he listened closely he could hear the voices off in the distance, straining not to yell. He knew they were different than before, but did not know why.

Stepping into the room, he searched for any clues to Isabel's whereabouts, but found nothing. He knelt on the floor in the position he had memorized as the spot where Alex had died.

"This is new," her voice said from behind him.

Snapping to his feet, Kyle found the object of his mission into his mind, standing in the doorway. "Isabel!"

"Good to see you've grown up," she said, obviously believing him to be just another dream image—which he was, in a way. "Does that mean you're ready to discuss why I'm here?"

"Isabel, it's me, Kyle," he said. "I've come to get you out."

"You're the one keeping me here." She still thought she was playing into the dream story line. "Let me go."

"No, Isabel." Kyle tried to clear up the confusion. "It's me. Kyle. Max sent me back into my dream to find you and bring you out."

"Kyle. Thank God!" She reached out and grabbed him in a joyful embrace. "How do we get out of here?"

"That's the funny thing," he said. "I'm not so sure."

"Let me get this straight," she said. "You came in here to rescue me, but there was no plan to get you back out?"

"It seemed like a good idea at the time. . . ." He knew just how dumb that sounded.

"Kyle!"

"We're trying," he defended the plan. "I realize you visit

people in their dreams all the time, but this is kind of uncharted territory for me."

"How long have I been in your mind?"

"It's almost two in the afternoon," he said, giving her a moment to let that information sink in.

"Eleven hours," she whispered in shock.

Kyle sat down on his bed and noticed it was much more comfortable in his dreams than in reality. "Have you been having a good time?"

"Kyle, your mind is one scary place," she said with a laugh, joining him on the bed. "But I think I've figured out why you're plagued with these dreams."

"What? How?"

"I've been stuck here with the Kyle Valenti version of Mini-Me," Isabel explained. "He showed me some interesting things."

"Like what?" Kyle asked.

"Here, let me show you," she replied, getting back up. "I think that may be the only way out of here." Taking Kyle by the hand, she led him through his house to the front door. When she glanced back at him, Kyle gave her a half-hearted smile to let her know he was ready for whatever they were about to do.

As Isabel opened the front door, she expected to be taken to the police station, since that seemed to be the order of things, but instead she found herself in the middle of the desert once again. "I thought I had things figured out," she mumbled to herself.

"I know this place," Kyle said.

"I was hoping you would," she replied. "Since it is your dream."

Kyle walked around, surveying the area, trying to remember why it was so familiar. It was more than just a dream image. There was a familiarity of years past, as if it were a memory from his childhood.

He dropped to his knees at exactly the same spot where Isabel and little Kyle had been digging the hole in which she found Alex. The earth was now undisturbed, since their earlier work had been wiped away.

"Go ahead," she prompted, hoping they would find a different "treasure" this time.

Kyle started digging with a manic pace, but it only took a few scoops of dirt before he hit something. Pushing away the soil, he pulled out a wooden box, holding it with two hands. It looked like a miniature version of a treasure chest from old pirate movies.

Isabel leaned in, hoping to see what was inside, but Kyle just sat staring at it, unable to lift the lid. She noticed it wasn't locked. It was only Kyle's own reluctance that kept him from opening the box.

"It was my sixth birthday," he said with his eyes locked on the box. "My dad was already at work when I woke up, but my mom was waiting in the kitchen for me. She said she had found a treasure map and we were going in search of buried treasure."

Isabel sat on the ground beside her friend to get comfortable for his story, hoping it would contain the answers they were waiting for.

"I was so excited," he continued, smiling. "I nearly made myself sick eating breakfast so quickly. After I got dressed, Mom got us into the car and we drove out here. It felt like it took forever."

He looked over to the side of the road and saw his mom's old car sitting there. A flash of recognition came over him because he had forgotten what it looked like. It had been so long since he had seen it pulling away.

"As soon as she stopped the car, I was out the door like a shot." He stared intently at the wooden box, as if it held all the answers. "Mom had to call me back to look at the map. I was ready to dig anywhere."

Kyle stood up, carrying the closed box with him. Isabel stood as well and followed her friend as he moved to a newly appeared mile marker planted by the side of the road.

"The map started here." He tapped his foot on the ground beside the marker. "Then, it led us in this direction twenty-five paces." Whispering, Kyle counted off as he walked to the collection of boulders that Isabel had used for shelter earlier. "From here, we went thirty paces north," he said, and walked the steps, with Isabel in tow, "until we wound up here." They were standing over the hole. "It took me forever to dig, even though it was hardly deep at all. And I found this."

Kyle opened the box.

As soon as light hit the contents, two screaming voices exploded around them, but this time it was not Tess and Alex. This time, they heard the angry shouts of Jim Valenti and a woman Isabel assumed to be Kyle's mom, Michelle.

Ignoring the voices since their words were unclear, Isabel peered into the box along with Kyle. Inside, she saw a baseball like the one little Kyle had been tossing earlier. But this one was different. This one had blue writing all over it.

"A signed baseball?" Isabel asked, incredulous.

"Signed by the nineteen eight-eight World Series champion Dodgers," Kyle clarified with reverence. "The richest treasure any boy could ask for. And I went and lost it, so long ago."

"That's why we're here?" Isabel shouted angrily. "A stupid baseball?" She certainly hoped there was more to the story, and expected there was a considerable amount of information yet to be shared.

"No," he replied, confirming her suspicions. "We're here because of that."

Looking up, they saw a police vehicle in the place where his mom's car had been. The red and blue lights weren't flashing, but there was an urgency about the vehicle nonetheless. Something about its very existence implied that they needed to hurry.

But Kyle was in no mood to hurry as he continued his tale, quietly counting off the paces in his mind as he headed for the car. The baseball was firmly in his hand, the box gone and forgotten. "Mom was supposed to pick me up after school."

"On your birthday?" Isabel asked for clarification.

"No," he said in a monotone. "This was later."

"Go on," she pressed as they reached the car.

"She always picked me up after school," he continued, staring at the ball. "Other kids took the bus, but my mom was there for me every day. Except one."

They got into the backseat of the car, but went nowhere. No one was in the driver's seat, although Isabel suspected that little detail didn't matter. If Kyle wanted the car to move, it would move.

"I waited a long time." Kyle looked out the window to the spot where he had found his treasure. "All the buses left, and all the other parents had come and gone. I was totally alone when Deputy Blackwood pulled up. I knew something was wrong."

Kyle reopened the door of the police car, and when he and Isabel got out, they were no longer in the desert. The car had deposited them right in front of the police station. The younger version of Deputy Blackwood Isabel had dealt with earlier walked in front of them, leading them into the station.

Phones were ringing. Voices overlapped one another. A young deputy holding a phone called Deputy Blackwood over to the front desk.

"Wait right here," the deputy said without looking back to them.

But Kyle ignored the deputy's words and continued walking the familiar route to his father's office, silently counting the steps as he walked.

Isabel followed, knowing they were on the verge of a breakthrough.

Once they reached the closed door to the office, Kyle stopped. They could hear the sheriff on the other side. He was crying.

"Aren't you going to open it?" Isabel asked hopefully.

"No," he said, staring at his empty hands.

"Where did the ball go?" she asked.

"I threw it out," he replied.

"When?" she prodded.

"As soon as I got home." He was stone-faced. "My dad told me that my mom had left while I was at school. That she wasn't coming back. At first I blamed him because he was the one telling me. By the time I got home, I was angry with her. I was so mad that I threw out the baseball she had given me on my birthday. It was the last truly happy time I had spent alone with her, and I didn't want to remember it."

"So you locked it away in your mind." Isabel felt they had almost solved his problem, and had braced herself to be flung from Kyle's mind.

"No." Kyle dashed her hopes. "I tried to forget it . . . to forget her. But the more I tried, the more I remembered. I know my dad got the ball out of the trash and put it away in a closet somewhere, but I've never found it. I've never looked."

The sheriff's sobs grew louder, echoing into the hallway.

Confused, Isabel pressed on. "Open the door, Kyle."

"No."

"Why not?"

He finally looked up into Isabel's eyes. "Big boys don't cry."

"But your father was crying," Isabel carefully pressed on.

"Big boys don't cry," he insisted, stern-faced.

"Kyle, open the door." She reached for his shoulder to provide emotional support.

Without breaking eye contact, Kyle held out his hand and turned the knob, opening the door.

They were both surprised to find that his bedroom was waiting for them on the other side.

The crying had stopped. His father was gone.

Stepping into the room, they found Alex's dead body lying on the floor, and paused for a moment in regret.

"What is it, Kyle?" she finally asked, sensing they were finally near the truth. "What is it you're not telling me?"

"Alex died on my birthday," Kyle said, grasping for answers. "The day before, actually."

In all the confusion surrounding Alex's death, Isabel could understand that she and her friends didn't remember to celebrate the occasion, but she could not figure out the link. "But what does this have to do with your nightmares? What do Alex and your mom have in common?"

Kyle stood, staring down at the body.

Isabel's mind raced. They kept getting closer to the solution to the puzzle, but she would have to force it out of him. "We're trapped in here because of you, Kyle. What is it you won't remember? What is it you refuse to accept?"

He dropped to the floor beside the body, with tears welling in his eyes. His own body heaved with convulsions.

Isabel was frightened to see her friend in such a state. He was in total breakdown. This was worse than anything she could have experienced in the real world, since it wasn't truly her friend Kyle doubled over in front of her. She was witnessing the mental manifestation of Kyle's breakdown. It was pure emotion being released without restraint. Nothing in life could ever come close to the pain she felt emanating from his body. His face twisted in agony.

Looking up at Isabel, he finally let out sobs for the years of repressing a single, seemingly minor, memory. "I carried her duffel bag to the car," he cried.

"What?" she asked, confused.

Suddenly, the sobs stopped and Kyle grew very still.

"We were leaving for school," he explained with a few rogue tears rolling down his face, "and I saw her bag. She told me she was going away for a while, but she never let on that it was for good. The bag was almost as big as me, but I picked it up and carried it for her. She said I was her strong, big boy."

Isabel was moved to tears by the recollection.

"I helped Tess take away Alex's body," Kyle finally let out the truth, "and I helped my mom abandon her family."

Dropping beside him, Isabel held on to her friend. "You had nothing to do with it, Kyle. You didn't cause Alex's death. You didn't make your mom leave. Both things would have happened whether or not you were there."

"But I could have stopped them," he argued, sobbing. "I could have stopped Tess. I could have stopped my mom."

"No, Kyle," Isabel soothed him. "You didn't have the power to stop either of them. You were just an innocent bystander caught up in it all."

"But—"

"No!" she said firmly. "You were the victim."

"I couldn't have stopped them?" His voice was child-like. It was the first time his mind was beginning to embrace the concept.

"No," Isabel pressed. "You were just a little boy. Even if you had realized what was going on, you couldn't have done anything about it. Just like if you had realized Tess was killing Alex, you couldn't have stopped her. You didn't have the power in either situation. There was nothing you could do."

"Nothing?" his voice continued in a child's tone.

"Nothing."

Alex's body began to fade. They both watched it intently, both contented and just a little sad to see him go away.

"I'm so tired," Kyle said with tears flowing freely once again.

Isabel pulled him up onto the bed. "Get some rest."

Kyle lay on his bed, curling himself into a ball.

Isabel took the covers from the foot of the bed and gently draped them over her friend. She stroked his hair as he began to look relaxed for the first time in a while. "It's going to be all right, Kyle. Everything's going to be all right."

20

In the Evanses' living room, Max watched as Jason started a rousing game of Jenga with Michael. The pair were crawling around on the floor picking up the pieces they had spilled out of the box and were carrying on like they were the ones who were old friends.

"I've never seen Michael warm up to a child so quickly," Max said as Maria came over to him.

"I've never seen him warm up to *anyone* so quickly," Maria agreed. "So, what's the kid's story?"

"Too long to go into," he replied.

"Gotcha," she said. "I think I'll join in the game."

Max continued to watch as she plopped herself on the floor beside Jason. For the first time that afternoon he was actually glad that he had brought the boy along. Considering the mood he and Liz had been greeted with yesterday, Max suspected this was probably the first bit of fun Jason had experienced in a while. He was also glad to have brought Jason for slightly selfish reasons as well, because the boy was providing a minor distraction for him to keep his mind off all the many frighteningly different things that could possibly be going wrong in the other room.

He continued to be amazed by how quickly Michael and Jason had bonded, although he suspected he shouldn't have been too surprised. Michael had spent years being roughed up by his foster father, Hank, all the while Max and Isabel were ignorant of the abuse. Somehow, Max suspected that the common bond between Michael and Jason was subtle enough that the pair would be naturally drawn to each other without realizing why. Max made a mental note to ask Michael about it some other time, then scratched it right off his mind when he remembered that Michael was never really big on those touchy-feely conversations.

Feeling silly standing in the doorway watching his friends playing, Max went over to join them on the floor. His mind wouldn't be even partially on the game, but at least it was a way to pass the time. The four of them settled into one of the quietest games of Jenga any of them had ever played. Three of the players kept an ear out to hear if they were needed in the other room while the fourth sensed the tension and remained mostly quiet out of respect.

Once Jason had finished placing the rows of rectangular blocks on top of one another, they took turns removing a block from the middle of the stack and placing it back on top. They went around the circle twice before Michael knocked it over, though Max suspected that the fall was on purpose since Jason was next and the tower was already leaning. *That is not the Michael Guerin I know,* Max thought. *But then again, I've never really seen him interacting with kids. Maybe there's a fun uncle in there for my son after all.*

Game play continued as the tower was rebuilt and they started again. The game still didn't take anyone's mind off Isabel and Kyle, but it did allow them to get more into it as the minutes passed. In fact, they were so engrossed in the game at one point that they didn't notice they were no longer alone.

Isabel and Liz had entered the room, stopping to watch them for a moment.

"Good to know I was missed," Isabel said quietly as she saw the game players on the floor. *Glad Max didn't have to interrupt his baby-sitter,* she thought as she noticed the young boy with them.

Liz let out a cough to discreetly announce their presence, but it was unfortunately timed with another fall of the Jenga tower and all four players bursting out in near riotous laughter.

"Good morning," Isabel said loudly from the doorway in a slightly annoyed tone. "I'm so glad that while Kyle and I were in there fighting for our lives and his sanity, you guys got to play some fun party games."

The look of relief on everyone's face was quite evident as Max was the first up to embrace his sister. The rest of the gang followed, although Jason stayed behind on the floor feeling somewhat out of place.

"Are you okay?" Max asked, squeezing tightly.

"Fine, I think," she said, stifling a yawn. "Surprisingly well rested, in fact."

"How's Kyle?" Maria asked.

"Resting comfortably," Liz said cheerily.

"He was still sleeping soundly," Isabel added. "We decided he needed the rest, so we didn't bother to wake him."

"Yeah," Liz agreed. "He's kind of taken over your room, Max. Sorry."

"Giving up my bed is the least I could do for him," Max replied. "Considering all the things he's been through."

"So what was the deal?" Michael asked bluntly.

Isabel didn't even consider explaining things, since she felt what they had gone through was Kyle's business and it wasn't her place to tell. "Just helping him battle some personal demons."

"Guess that means we can go," Michael said quickly, giving Isabel a hug to welcome her back to the waking world. "I for one could use a shower."

"Me too," Max, Maria, Isabel, and even Jason all said in unison.

"Call us if you go to any other planes of existence," Maria added in Isabel's ear so she wouldn't be overheard.

"I'll walk you to the door," Isabel said, leading them away. "Thanks for your help, guys."

"No problem," Maria said. "Just another typical day in Roswell."

"Oh, for the atypical day every now and then," Isabel said.

"From your lips," Maria agreed as they reached the front door. "Oh, some guy from your dad's work stopped by. Kyle spoke to him."

"Jesse?" Isabel slipped before she remembered to play ignorant. While she had been stuck in Kyle's head she had not entirely forgotten about their plans to get together, but it had slipped to the back of her mind. Now that she was finally free, it became her primary concern. She could only hope that he would forgive her for blowing him off two times in as many days. But then again, it was a good measuring stick for their relationship since she suspected this would not be the last time her other life would get in the way.

"Kyle didn't mention his name," Maria said with growing suspicion over this mystery man. "He told the guy that you were sick. I thought you should know in case he calls or something."

"Thanks," Isabel said, looking for a way to change the subject.

"We should go," Michael said bluntly, unknowingly coming to his friend's rescue.

"Don't you just love those temperamental artists?" Maria commented to Isabel cryptically. "Let's go, Rembrandt."

"I don't know why I ever tell you anything," he said, although Isabel had no idea what they were talking about.

"You never tell me anything," Maria reminded him.

"Well, thanks again." Isabel ushered them out the open door. "We must do this again some time."

"Until the next crisis," Maria agreed.

"Until then," Isabel said.

"Yeah. Bye," the king of the monosyllabic sentence added.

Isabel watched as the pair made their way down the front walk. *No matter what evidence we may have to the contrary,* she thought, *those two were made for each other. No one else will have them.*

As Isabel was saying good-bye to their friends, Max and Liz rejoined Jason on the floor, cleaning up the scattered wood pieces and returning them to the box from which they had come.

"Your sister looks like she's feeling better," Jason said.

"Yeah, we think it was a twenty-four-hour flu," Max replied. "She got it the same time yesterday, and apparently it's very precise."

Jason looked at him like he didn't know what to make of what Max was saying. That is until both Max and Liz started giggling.

"Sorry this weekend got so crazy," Liz said.

"Are you kidding?" Jason's eyes went wide. "I was rescued from a mine shaft, got to visit the place I grew up, met all your cool friends, *and* kicked Michael's butt in Jenga. This was, like, the best weekend ever." He had the first genuine smile on his face that Max had seen all weekend. "I never want to go home."

The look of seriousness that crossed Liz's and Max's faces told him that was not an option. The expression was contagious as the smile was wiped away from his face as well. The distractions had served their purpose in getting him to forget his troubles, but all three of them knew that there was still a long way to go before the situation was finally resolved.

Liz took his hand, "We'll talk to your mom together. And I'll even stay until we go back to the doctor on Monday."

"Yeah, whatever." The carefree Jason of the past hour had disappeared.

"Don't worry," Liz said. "Aunt Jackie will take care of everything."

The silence that followed was enough to tell Max all that he needed to know.

"Your mom already knows, doesn't she," Max spoke his suspicions.

"I never told her," Jason reluctantly admitted. "But, yeah. She has to know."

Liz was beside herself. "I can't believe Aunt Jackie—"

Max grabbed her free hand, giving her a gentle look that said *not now.* "New plan," he said, focusing his attention back to Jason. "We'll take you to see Liz's mom. I suspect if there's anyone who can get through to your mom, it will be her."

The look of hope on Jason's face nearly made both Max's and Liz's hearts break. "You think?"

"Absolutely," Liz said firmly. "My mom will make sure Aunt Jackie accepts the truth. And if she can't . . . I've always wanted to have a little brother."

It seemed so simple, but Max knew that it wouldn't be. He also knew how important Jason was to Liz, and that made the boy important to him as well. They would see to it that Jason was protected, even if it meant bringing Max's own father and his law firm in on it.

"I do have one question, though," Max said.

Jason looked uncomfortable. "What?"

"Back at the ranch," he asked, "what happened to all the sheep?"

Jason laughed out loud as he detailed the story of the missing sheep by explaining that the rules of George's inheritance from his parents had required him to look after the sheep for six years. The time limit was up two months ago, and the sheep went with it.

"That's it?" Liz sounded disappointed. "I was hoping for something more."

"Sorry," Jason replied.

"And who have we got here?" Isabel asked, coming back into the room.

"Jason," Max performed the introductions, "this is my sister, Isabel. Isabel, this is my friend Jason."

"Nice to meet you," Isabel said, giving the boy's hand a shake.

"Hi," he stammered with an odd look on his face. "Glad you're feeling better."

"Thanks." She smiled. "Well, if you don't mind, I've got a phone call to make." She grabbed the cordless phone as Jason's eyes followed her every move.

"We were on our way out." Max watched Jason watch his sister. "I may be home later this afternoon, depending on things."

Isabel silently cursed her dumb luck. "Well, since I've been cooped up all morning, I might go out tonight, so I'll see you later." She was out of the room before he could ask her anything about her plans.

"Well, we should get over to Liz's place," Max said, noticing that Jason's eyes were still locked in the direction Isabel had just gone. "And maybe you and I should continue that conversation about changes that we started last night," he added in a conspiratorial whisper.

"I call the front seat," Jason yelled as he ran out to the car, slightly embarrassed.

"He's a good kid." Max took Liz's hand as they also walked out to the car.

"So, do you have any more fears about raising your own son?" she asked.

Her gave her hand a little squeeze. "I'm sure I always will. But as long as I have you around to help me out, I have a good feeling that everything will be just fine."

He leaned in to kiss her, feeling secure in the knowledge that he would get his son back one day. With Liz by his side, not only did he think he would be fine raising his child, but he felt secure in the knowledge that he was growing up and into the role of the leader that he had been born to fill.

Back in the house, Isabel stopped in the doorway to Max's room before continuing on to her own. Checking in on Kyle, she saw that he appeared to be sleeping peacefully, all curled up in the fetal position.

Since there was a shadow across his face, she couldn't be sure, but it appeared that he was sucking his thumb. She could, however, see his right hand clearly and, unlike the previous night, she could tell that it was completely still. The tapping had ceased and she expected that the dreams had stopped as well. She smiled at the sight, hoping that, for a while at least, Kyle and all her friends would have nothing but pleasant dreams.

EPILOGUE

Summer was back with a vengeance.

The cool weather had broken, and early Sunday morning it was already ten degrees hotter than Saturday's high. Isabel hardly felt the heat, however, as she climbed the hill. Max had lent her his car since he was spending the day with Jason, Liz, and her family before they all went back to Artesia together to speak with Jason's mom. Even though she knew the car could make it up the hill, she did not wish to disturb the quiet, tranquil setting and had left it behind at the bottom.

Brushing away a bead of perspiration, Isabel knelt on the ground with a bouquet of sunflowers laid out before her. She always found sunflowers to be the most interesting variety of flora. To look at them, they certainly weren't as pretty as roses, lilies, or even carnations, but their bright color and sturdy look always cheered her up when she was down, much in the way a particular friend used to have a similar effect on her.

She'd had a wonderful date with Jesse the night before,

once they'd managed to avoid running into Kyle and his dad as the pair were out to dinner together at the same place she had chosen to go. Jesse had been totally understanding of her blowing him off because of her fake illness, too. Just another lie in the dozens she had told to friends and loved ones. But, somehow, it felt wrong to be thinking of Jesse, considering where she was at the moment.

"This is a nice surprise," a voice came from behind her.

"What? After yesterday, you didn't expect to see me here?"

"Well, yeah, but it's still nice to see you." His voice was drawing her in. "It would be nicer to be *seen* by you."

"I can't," she said, her eyes firmly fixed to his tombstone. His name . . . Alex Whitman. Born . . . 1983. Died . . . *too young.*

"I think I'm pretty good looking," he said, "all things considered."

Isabel tried not to smile at the gallows humor. "You know what I mean. It hurts too much to look at you . . . after seeing how you died."

"You'd rather remember me like that?" he asked. "Doubled over in pain? Begging for—"

"Stop!" she cried. "I don't want to remember it at all."

"You have to," he said. "It's the price you pay for helping Kyle."

"No good deed ever goes unpunished."

"Isabel." She could feel his breath on her shoulder even though it was not real. "Look at me."

She finally turned to see Alex, or at least the image of Alex. He looked just as she remembered him, with the same goofball smile he always had plastered onto his face. She loved that smile because she knew it had always gotten just a little brighter whenever he'd noticed she was in the room. This was not his first visit to her since his death, and she had hoped it would not be his last. She wasn't sure if he was a ghost, a dream, or something else entirely, but Isabel didn't care.

"I know it was hard to watch me die," Alex said. "Trust me, I was there." Even in death, his pitiful attempts at humor would still elicit a sad smile from her. "But now, knowing you were there too . . . it makes my death a little less lonely. It took so long for us to really get together in life, and now I feel like we were also a little bit together in death. If anything, it makes us closer."

"I miss you so much." She had a tear in her eye.

"I'm never far," he said. "You know that."

"I know," she replied. "And I'm glad."

"Good, now stop being such a mope," he smiled. "This place is depressing enough as it is. Everyone's crying when they come here. And if they're not crying, they're really quiet, as if they would wake anyone. What I wouldn't give for The Whits to make an unscheduled appearance."

"That reminds me," she said, smiling for the first time. "We did that talent night that you, Maria, and Liz had every year." Isabel proceeded to tell him all about the evening's festivities. It didn't matter that he wasn't really standing in front of her, or that if he was actually a ghost, then he probably already knew everything she was saying. It just felt good for Isabel to be talking to him. In fact, she continued talking for a good half hour, updating Alex on almost every part of her life, although she left the whole Jesse thing out of it, not wanting to spoil the mood. By the time she had covered just about every subject, the sun had pumped up the temperature by a few more degrees, making it a little more uncomfortable.

A gentle breeze blew up the hill, cooling Isabel. She half suspected that Alex had arranged for the breeze to cool her. He had always been trying to take care of her in life, so it would stand to reason that he would continue to do so in death. Maybe he was going to become her own personal guardian angel. *I could think of worse people to have watching over me,* she thought.

"Thanks, Alex," she said, wrapping up their conversation. "It's good to have a friend to talk to."

"You have plenty of friends," Alex reminded her.

"But none of them understands me like you did," she said, standing up and smoothing the wrinkles out of her sundress. "Like you *do.* None of them cares like you."

A bluebird swooped out of the sky and landed on his tombstone. It perched itself along the edge as if wanting to be a spectator as the scene played itself out.

"I should get going," she said as she turned herself in the direction of Max's car, preparing for the long walk back down but not really wanting to go yet, for a number of reasons.

"Really?" he asked, feigning surprise. "Before you say what it is that you came here to say?"

"I just wanted to see you," she said, lying to both Alex and herself. "You know . . . after yesterday."

"Who exactly do you think you're fooling?" he asked. "I know what's going on in your beautiful, yet pleasantly complicated head. There's something else. Something you want to say to me."

She was almost too afraid to speak, but managed to get out a "Yes."

"A suspicion," he prodded. "Something that you can't bring yourself to say out loud on your own."

"It's probably nothing," she replied. "This crazy life. It makes me paranoid."

"True." He smiled again. "But you still have to say it. Just to hear the words spoken. Just so they can stop running over and over in your mind."

She knew he was right. Whether the ghost of Alex was actually standing beside her didn't matter. The fact that it *was* probably just her overactive imagination was also unimportant. She had to speak the thought that had been nagging her since yesterday or else she would now be the one not getting any sleep.

Bracing herself for hearing her own words, Isabel finally spoke them aloud. "Kyle's mom left Roswell when he was six years old."

"Go on."

"She left around the same time we came out of the pods."

And there they were.

Isabel knew that she could not pursue that line of thought with anyone else. At best, it would open up old wounds while at worst it could lead to even more tragic consequences. And if she had learned anything from her experience with Kyle, it was to not obsess about the past.

She stole one last look at her friend standing by his gravestone. His hands rested casually in his pockets. The smile on his face filled her with a level of peacefulness that she had not felt since before his death. She carried that image of Alex with her as she walked back down the hill, heading for home.

ABOUT THE AUTHOR

Paul Ruditis used to work in Hollywood, where he was surrounded by people who seemed to be from other planets. He has written and contributed to several books based on such notable TV shows as *Buffy the Vampire Slayer*; *Sabrina, the Teenage Witch*; *Enterprise*; and *The West Wing*. He is also the author of *Roswell Pop Quiz*.